# The Cowboys Runaway Bride

## Nancy Robards Thompson

 HARLEQUIN®SPECIAL EDITION®

If you purchased this book without a cover you should be aware that this book is stolen property. It was reported as "unsold and destroyed" to the publisher, and neither the author nor the publisher has received any payment for this "stripped book."

Recycling programs
for this product may
not exist in your area.

ISBN-13: 978-0-373-62322-8

The Cowboy's Runaway Bride

Copyright © 2016 by Nancy Robards Thompson

All rights reserved. Except for use in any review, the reproduction or utilization of this work in whole or in part in any form by any electronic, mechanical or other means, now known or hereinafter invented, including xerography, photocopying and recording, or in any information storage or retrieval system, is forbidden without the written permission of the publisher, Harlequin Enterprises Limited, 225 Duncan Mill Road, Don Mills, Ontario M3B 3K9, Canada.

This is a work of fiction. Names, characters, places and incidents are either the product of the author's imagination or are used fictitiously, and any resemblance to actual persons, living or dead, business establishments, events or locales is entirely coincidental.

This edition published by arrangement with Harlequin Books S.A.

For questions and comments about the quality of this book, please contact us at CustomerService@Harlequin.com.

® and TM are trademarks of Harlequin Enterprises Limited or its corporate affiliates. Trademarks indicated with ® are registered in the United States Patent and Trademark Office, the Canadian Intellectual Property Office and in other countries.

Printed in U.S.A.

www.Harlequin.com

FORT WORTH LIBRARY

3 1668 06968 8122

**"If you know ⎯⎯⎯⎯⎯⎯⎯⎯⎯⎯⎯⎯⎯
break in?"**

"She was supposed to leave me a key, but I couldn't find it."

He squinted at her. "Where was she supposed to leave it?"

"Under a planter. She wasn't specific, and, as I said, I couldn't find it. That's when I saw the open window—"

Ethan held up his hand, silencing her.

"Just give me your cell phone."

"I don't have it on my person."

His mouth twisted in a dubious expression and he grunted. "On your *person*? I've been giving you the benefit of the doubt. If you don't want to cooperate, I can call Joyce back and we can sort out what's what down at the station."

He held out his hand again, this time moving his fingers in a "give it to me" gesture.

"It's in the car." Now he was starting to irritate her. "I'm certainly not hiding it." She ran her hands down the silhouette of her body to emphasize that she was wearing a T-shirt and a rather snug skirt that didn't leave room for secret pockets.

When she realized that Ethan Campbell's gaze was meandering the same path her own hands had traced she regretted issuing the invitation.

**CELEBRATION, TX:**
**Love is just a celebration away...**

Dear Reader,

I've always admired people who knew exactly what they wanted to do with their lives. My mother knew she wanted to be a nurse from age four. Not only did she fulfill that dream, she had a long and prosperous career. Sadly, I didn't inherit the gene of career certainty from her. I changed my major three times before earning my degree in journalism. After I got my diploma, I changed jobs several times before I realized that my calling was writing fiction. Now I can't imagine doing anything else, but I did take the long way around the barn getting here.

It took Chelsea Ashford Alden, the heroine of *The Cowboy's Runaway Bride*, a while to figure out her calling, too. Talk about taking the long way around the barn! Chelsea had to travel all the way from England to Celebration, Texas, to figure out her future. Fate was smiling on her, because not only did she find the space she needed to figure out her mind in Celebration, she met horse breeder Ethan Campbell, the love of her life. What's not to love about a big, strong cowboy who proved he'd go to the ends of the earth to protect his lady love?

I hope you enjoy Ethan and Chelsea's story as much as I enjoyed writing it. Please find me on Facebook at Facebook.com/nrobardsthompson, on Twitter at @NRTWrites or drop me a line at nrobardsthompson@yahoo.com. I love to hear from readers!

Warmly,

*Nancy*

National bestselling author **Nancy Robards Thompson** holds a degree in journalism. She worked as a newspaper reporter until she realized reporting "just the facts" bored her silly. Now that she has much more content to report to her muse, Nancy loves writing women's fiction and romance full-time. Critics have deemed her work "funny, smart and observant." She resides in Florida with her husband and daughter. You can reach her at nancyrobardsthompson.com and Facebook.com/nancyrobardsthompsonbooks.

Visit the Author Profile page at Harlequin.com for more titles.

This book is dedicated to Katherine Garbera
for helping me dream up the heroine of
*The Cowboy's Runaway Bride*
and for your unwavering friendship.
Kathy, you're the sister of my heart.

## *Chapter One*

Lady Chelsea Ashford Alden cast a wary glance over her shoulder as she approached the front door of the gray stone cottage.

The place looked dark and formidable—cold and utterly unwelcoming—like it didn't want to be friends. It was so contrary to her university roommate Juliette Lowell's vibrant personality. Hard to believe Juliette lived here. However, in the dark, Chelsea could see the numbers on the house matched the address her friend had given her.

The fingernail of moon hanging high in the inky Texas sky wasn't her friend, either. It did nothing to light the porch. Then again, maybe the darkness was her best ally, cloaking her in shadows, hiding her from the monster that had sent her running to Juliette for refuge in the first place.

Life as the Earl of Downing's daughter didn't offer much latitude or forgiveness. In fact, sometimes it seemed as if people were standing back and waiting for her to fall. When she didn't, others were looking for opportunities to pull the rug out from under her or stick out a leg to trip her up.

Which was why she was in Texas.

She was tired of the limelight; tired of the pomp and pretense; tired of people using her; tired of watching her life play out on the covers of the British tabloids. Because God knew what the paparazzi couldn't confirm, they invented or they paid off acquaintances to create stories for them. She had experienced that compliments of a reporter named Bertie Veal, who had stalked her since university.

Most recently, he'd colluded with her ex to ruin her life. There was no worse betrayal than when someone you trusted in the most intimate way sold your most vulnerable moment to the press.

Chelsea tried to blink away the image, but it was burned into her brain. Intimate footage she didn't know existed until it had appeared on the tabloid's website.

She shuddered at the thought as she lifted the welcome mat in search of the key Juliette had left for her. The video had set off a humiliating chain reaction, the worst of which was her father's embarrassment and disappointment.

The look on his face had been devastating. It had

cut her to the quick when he and her mother had told her she was on her own to solve the problem, that it was best for all if she distanced herself from the family until she'd cleaned up her mess—as if by virtue of simply leaving the country, London's upper crust would forget she was their daughter.

At least they would pretend to forget. In the meantime, it was very clear that Chelsea was cordially invited to stay away until she'd gotten her life together.

The first step in Plan Damage Control was to make freelance trash reporter Bertie Veal leave her alone. The only way she would accomplish that was to disappear. Celebration, Texas, was the perfect place to hide because it was the last place in the world anyone would think to look for her.

No one would recognize her here. Most Americans seemed interested in the Buckingham Palace royals. They didn't care about the antics of the two-bit daughter of an obscure earl. American tabloids were all about Charles and Camilla, Wills and Kate, or movie stars spotted without makeup and rap singers caught cheating.

Chelsea switched on her phone's flashlight app and shone it on the wooden floorboards, but found nothing.

She tried the door, but it was locked. Juliette was a wedding planner and she was in San Antonio on business this weekend. She'd made it clear that Chelsea was welcome and apologized for not being there when she arrived, but duty called.

After a wedding reception Jules had dreamed up

had been featured in Southern Living, her business had skyrocketed.

Chelsea was happy for her friend and glad that at least one of them had her life together. She assured Juliette she could manage, and they'd bid their temporary goodbyes with promises of a long catch-up as soon as Juliette got home.

The only logical hiding places for a key on the front porch were the doormat and a rocking chair. Again, she used the flashlight feature on her phone to search around the chair, but she came away empty-handed.

Perhaps Jules had left it on the back porch. They'd been in such a hurry when they'd talked that only now did it dawn on Chelsea that Jules hadn't mentioned a specific location for the key—only that she would leave it on the porch. Or maybe Chelsea had misunderstood. How hard could it be to find a hidden key?

The flash of headlights warned of an approaching car. Chelsea sank back into the shadows, deciding she was grateful for the cloak of darkness that concealed her. As the vehicle continued to move down the road she breathed a sigh of relief.

After the car was gone, she made her way to the back of the house away from the street to see if she could locate another hiding spot for the key.

When Chelsea and Juliette had roomed together at university, the two had weathered stronger forces than Bertie Veal. Well, nothing worse than discovering Hadden Hastings, her ex-boyfriend, had sold a video he'd secretly recorded of Chelsea and him having sex, but she and Jules had gotten into their share of trouble over the years. If they hadn't been knee-deep in it together, they'd gone to great lengths to cover for each other. That was what made them such good friends.

When Chelsea had phoned Juliette and told her she was in trouble and had given her the bare-bones rundown of Hadden's betrayal, she'd insisted Chelsea seek refuge with her in Celebration.

Chelsea and Juliette had both known Hadden Hastings at university. He'd been part of their group of friends. But Chelsea hadn't dated him until the year after they'd graduated.

When she ran into him after she got home from a year of doing relief aid work in Africa, she'd seen him with different eyes. He'd suddenly become datable. He'd been fun and funny and romantic and sympathetic to her post-university quandary—after all, he couldn't seem to find his place in the world, either.

He'd charmed her and she'd fallen for him.

He was the last person she'd ever thought would secretly record their lovemaking, much less sell the footage to Bertie Veal. The betrayal hurt as much as the humiliation of having a "sex tape" published for the entire world to view. The press ate it up because there was nothing quite as titillating as a noble scandal.

Chelsea lifted up the mat at the back door and ran her hand over the rough surface of the wooden floorboard.

Nothing. No key there, either.

Then she lifted up the various flowerpots and tipped the planters, all to no avail. As a last resort, she called Juliette, but the call went straight to voice mail.

"Hello, Jules. It's Chelsea. I'm so sorry to bother you because you're probably knee-deep in first dances and cake cuttings right now. But I made it to your house and I can't locate the key. Please give me a quick ring when you have a moment. It's probably in some painfully obvious place that I'm not seeing. You know me." She forced a laugh. "Anyhow, I hope the wedding is going well. I can't wait to see you. Toodles, love."

She disconnected the call and was just about ready to give up and return to the car when she noticed that a small window near the back door was open a few inches.

It wasn't optimal, but it was a way inside.

The window was small—tiny, in fact—and a bit high off the ground. And why had she chosen to wear a skirt today? Well, it didn't matter now. It wasn't as if anyone was lurking about, hoping to catch a glimpse of her knickers.

Chelsea stared up at the window and sighed.

It appeared to be her last recourse. She could either make it work or wait in the car until Juliette called her back. It was getting chilly out here. She'd much rather wait snug and safe inside.

She dragged over a patio chair made out of fat plastic pipe with a woven nylon seat base and positioned it under the window. Kicking off her wedge sandals, she tucked her phone and rental car key into one shoe and climbed up onto the chair. It wobbled a bit and she grabbed the window ledge to steady herself.

Chelsea was a solid five foot nine inches in bare feet. Hoisting herself up and inside that tiny window would be a challenge, but this was no time to fret. She couldn't overthink it. The sooner she got inside the house, the sooner she could relax.

She got to work on removing the screen. It took more effort than she thought it would. In the process, she broke her right index fingernail into the quick, which smarted like bloody hell. The pain had her performing a little jig, which caused the chair to rock unsteadily. But a moment later Chelsea persevered and popped the window screen out of its track. It clattered as she dropped it onto the porch floor.

Now it was time for the most challenging feat of the evening: stuffing herself through the small opening. The window looked into a small bathroom and was positioned just above the bathtub. A double swag shower curtain framed the tub. Beyond that she could make out a commode and a pedestal sink. The door to the room seemed to open into a hallway, but that was all she could see in the dim light.

With one deep breath, Chelsea used all the arm strength she could muster to pull herself up. As she labored, she managed to get a foothold on the house's cold, gray stones and used them to walk herself up the wall.

She just might pull this off.

With one last grunt and upward push, she managed to tip herself inside the window…sort of… During the effort, her foot caught on the chair—how the bloody hell had that happened? If she'd tried to do that on purpose she wouldn't have been able to. Nonetheless, the chair seemed to be attached to her foot. With a swift kick and a smart shake, she managed to free her lower limb. The chair crashed to the ground, echoing in the otherwise silent night, and leaving her precariously half in, half out of the window, faltering like a teeter-totter trying to find its balance.

With her arse hanging out in the most undignified manner, she was sure there was a life metaphor hidden somewhere in this situation. But this was no time to ponder it. She was going to fall one way or the other, and after all the work it had taken to get this far, she wasn't about to start over.

With one last forward thrust, Chelsea tumbled inside. As she twisted to break her fall, the bathroom light flicked on. Chelsea screamed as she registered the huge man hulking in the threshold.

Based on the racket he'd heard, Ethan Campbell thought he might have cornered a couple of raccoons that had fallen down the chimney or gotten into Juliette Lowell's house through an open window. The last thing he'd expected was to catch a tall, gorgeous blonde breaking and entering.

But there she was looking guilty as hell, standing in the bathtub, tugging up on the neckline of her blouse and smoothing her bright pink skirt into place. The open window was a yawning black hole behind her.

With her wide eyes and tousled long hair, the Beatles' song, "She Came in Through The Bathroom Window," suddenly took on a whole new meaning. Ethan tried to ignore how pretty she was and stepped forward to show the woman he meant business.

There had been some burglaries in Celebration over the past few weeks. Was this woman part of a ring?

"What the hell do you think you're doing?" he asked.

He didn't wait for her to answer and he didn't take his eyes off her as he reached into his jeans' pocket for his phone to call the sheriff. She was barefoot, he noticed. He also registered her long, lean, tanned legs and the barely there hint of cleavage that winked at him as she crossed her arms.

He forced his gaze back to her face. She stared at him, big-eyed and mute. She looked scared, like a cornered cub. He had a hard time believing Goldilocks was here to ransack the place. Nonetheless, she wasn't supposed to be here.

No one was.

So what was she doing?

When he'd noticed the strange car parked in the Juliette Lowell's driveway as he'd headed home from the stables, Ethan decided to investigate.

Juliette was in San Antonio facilitating one of those fancy weddings people paid her good money to plan. That was why Ethan had decided to stop and investigate.

His neighbor kept him apprised of her travel schedule and that's why he knew damn good and well *no one* was supposed to be in this house tonight.

"I'll ask you again," he said, waiting to hear what she said before he dialed the sheriff. "You want to tell me what you're doing in here, sis?"

The woman stared back at him silently. Those huge eyes of hers—were they blue or green?—still locked with his.

"No?" he asked. "Okay. Maybe you'd rather talk to the cops?"

That broke her silence. "No, don't call the police. Please."

Did she have an accent? He couldn't tell. Might just be nerves.

She held up her hands surrender-style.

"Well, then you'd better start talking—and fast. Are you alone?"

*Aw, hell.* He was such an idiot. She could have accomplices. They might already be in the house. She could've been the lookout. Albeit, a noisy one. But still…

Ethan glanced in the mirror, which provided a side view into the dim hallway, and listened hard, trying to detect sound or movement, anything that indicated they weren't alone.

He didn't hear a thing.

Yeah, wouldn't it be just like him to meet his maker after being distracted by a pretty face. It wouldn't be the first time. Well, figuratively, anyway.

As a safeguard, he placed the call to 911.

"No! Please don't. My name is Chelsea—Chelsea

Allen. I'm here to visit my friend, Juliette Lowell. Please don't call the police. I can assure you that's not necessary. Just call Juliette. She'll tell you I'm welcome here. *Please*. Hang up. We don't need to involve the officials."

This time there was no trace of an accent in her voice. He must've imagined it before. Because now her words were crisp and enunciated. And panicked.

And she was so pretty.

*Oh, for the love of God almighty...*

She did know Juliette's name. Which didn't automatically guarantee that she was a friend. She might have known the house would be empty tonight and the place would be a good target.

Juliette's business was just starting to take off. She was even getting some press about it. Who knew what kind of riffraff news of her success might attract? Though Chelsea Allen didn't look like riffraff.

"Please hang up," she pleaded again.

Ethan shook his head and gestured to the window behind her. "When you visit friends, do you always enter through the bathroom?"

Her eyes flashed before she glanced over her shoulder in the direction he pointed. "Of course not. It's just that..."

A frustrated little growl gobbled up the rest of her words. Ethan half expected her to stamp her foot or to turn around and scale the wall in an attempt to leave the way she came in.

But instead, she put her hands on her hips and apparently tried to turn the tables on him. "If Juliette is not at home, what business do *you* have in her house? Who are *you*?"

He frowned at her tone. "I'm the one who's asking the questions here, and as soon as the sheriff arrives, he will take over for me."

"No! I'm sorry. Please hang up. I mean, you do realize that calling emergency services could keep them from responding to a true emergency, don't you? Just call Juliette from your cell. If you're in her house you should have her number. Right? She will tell you that we're friends and that I'm absolutely welcome here."

Ethan hesitated. She had a point. But before he could disconnect, the operator picked up.

"This is 911. What is your emergency?"

## Chapter Two

"Hey, Joyce, it's Ethan Campbell," he said. "False alarm on that 911."

Chelsea finally drew in a breath after she heard him retract the police call. *Ethan Campbell*. So that was his name. Chelsea racked her brain trying to recall if she'd ever heard Juliette mention him. Campbell... Sounded familiar. But the way he was glaring at her as he talked to the sheriff's dispatcher addled her mind and made it difficult to remember her own name, much less her college friend's list of boyfriends past.

"Nope. Everything's under control, but hang tight. I'll call you back if the situation changes."

Pinned by his midnight blue gaze, she stood frozen, weighing her options. At least she had enough sense to realize most of the choices sponsored by the

fight-or-flight adrenaline rush weren't very practical…
or smart—like grabbing the phone out of the guy's
hand and tossing it into the toilet or scaling the wall
and going out the way she'd come in.

Both plans spelled disaster.

If she did the grab and flush, Ethan Campbell
would probably lock her in the bathroom and call
the sheriff from Juliette's landline. The last thing she
needed was for the police to show up. Because where
the police went, media usually followed.

Of course, if he locked her in the bath, she could
climb back out the window. But she wasn't a gym-
nast or a contortionist. So she wouldn't be very fast.
She wasn't even remotely athletic. It had taken forever and every ounce of strength she'd possessed to
hoist herself up and climb in the window. Her muscles
were still shaky after being taxed the first time. She'd
be deluding herself if she thought she was capable of
using that route for a speedy and successful getaway.

Bloody hell, if she did escape, where would she go?

A chase would ensue; the cops would be on her
heels.

Maybe she could simply push past Ethan and make
a run out the front door. That seemed like the least
shady option. But there was no getting around him. He
was a big guy. Being tackled and held by those rugby-
player arms and pinned by those shoulders might have
been quite nice under other circumstances. But right
now his considerable bulk filled the doorway, blocking the only other viable exit, eliminating that option.

"Yeah, I thought I'd caught the burglar at the Lowell place," he drawled into the phone.

*Burglar?* Did she really look like someone who sneaked into homes and robbed people?

"Turns out it's a woman claiming to be a friend of Juliette's. Sit tight. I'm going to call her to confirm... No. I don't need backup. I got this."

Finally, they were getting somewhere.

He seemed to be quite familiar with her friend. Against her better judgment, Chelsea wondered why Juliette *hadn't* talked about this Ethan Campbell. He was tall and rugged and handsome—if you liked big, brooding, broad-shouldered men with Texas drawls.

And who in her right mind wouldn't find a guy like him attractive?

He'd be even better if he wasn't holding her hostage.

She reminded herself of that, and the fact that he seemed to be pretty well connected to the local authorities, which could be a problem. A *big problem* if he pressed her for personal information. That would mean she'd need to leave again because she couldn't take the chance of word getting out and Bertie tracking her here. Celebration was too small of a town to hide from a bloodhound like him. She was running out of options of where to go. Unless she wanted to hole up someplace alone. If she blew it here, it meant she'd have to go home.

That wasn't an option. At least not right now.

"If her story doesn't check out, I'll call you back and have you send the sheriff out."

Ethan was nodding at something the dispatcher was saying on the other end of the line.

"Joyce…" More talking. More nodding. "No. Joyce…It's fine…"

"Yes, I'm sure…No, I don't see anyone else with her. She's alone." He turned his gaze back on Chelsea. "Are you alone?"

Chelsea nodded and instantly regretted it. Maybe she shouldn't have said that. But if she hadn't they surely would've dispatched the authorities.

"Her car's out in the driveway…No. I didn't get the license number. It was dark when I got here. I wanted to make sure the perimeter was secured first."

Was the guy a wannabe cop or something?

More listening. More nodding. Chelsea strained to see if she could hear what the person on the other end of the line was saying, but all she could discern was a low hum of an indistinct feminine voice.

Ethan backed into the hallway and flicked on the overhead light. Now Chelsea could see a collage of black-and-white photographs housed in a multipaned black frame hanging on the wall behind him. One of the pictures was from Juliette's days at St. Andrew's, and as if by some miracle, there was a shot of her and Juliette and a group of their schoolmates huddled together at a Sussex rugby match.

"Good idea," he snarled into the phone. He turned to Chelsea and held out his hand. "Give me your cell."

"Why do you want my cell phone?" she asked.

Still pressing his phone to one ear, Ethan gestured with his free hand. "Phone."

Chelsea pointed to the photo behind him. Ethan squinted at her and shook his head.

"Look at the photograph behind you," she said, nodding in that direction.

When Ethan didn't immediately turn around, Chelsea said, "There's a photograph of Juliette and me on the wall over your right shoulder. If you'll simply turn around, you'll see I'm telling the truth."

With one last wary glance at Chelsea, Ethan cast a quick look behind him. He did a double take. "Hold on a sec, Joyce. Actually, I'll call you back if I need you."

After he disconnected the call, he said, "If you know Juliette so well, why did you break in?"

"She was supposed to leave me a key, but I couldn't find it."

He squinted at her. "Where was she supposed to leave it?"

"Under the doormat or someplace. She wasn't specific, and, as I said, I couldn't find it. That's when I saw the open window—"

Ethan held up his hand, silencing her.

"Give me your cell phone."

"I don't have it on my person at the moment."

His mouth twisted in a dubious expression and he grunted. "On your *person*? I've been giving you the benefit of the doubt. If you don't want to cooperate, I can call Joyce back and we can sort out what's what down at the station."

He held out his hand again, this time moving his fingers in a give-it-to-me gesture.

"It's outside on the back porch in one of my sandals." Now he was starting to irritate her. "I'm certainly not hiding it." She ran her hands down the silhouette of her body to emphasize that she was wearing a T-shirt and a rather snug skirt that didn't leave room for secret pockets.

When she realized that Ethan Campbell's gaze was meandering the same path her own hands had traced, she regretted issuing the invitation.

She cleared her throat and crossed her arms over the front of her body. "I tried to call Juliette, but she didn't answer. I left a message and then I saw the open window. I took off my sandals and set down my phone and car key before I came in through the window. If you'll check outside, you'll find everything."

She shrugged a jerky little motion to indicate her annoyance.

"Wouldn't it be better to just call Juliette's number from your own phone, anyway? I'm surprised you're not afraid that I might call one of my henchmen to come and break me out of here."

His brow shot up and she realized she'd probably said the wrong thing.

"You have henchmen?"

"That was supposed to be a joke."

"How about some identification?" he said, obviously not amused.

Great. Just great. If he saw the name on her ID, the cat could very possibly be out of the bag. Especially if he called the police back and gave her name to the sheriff. If they ran her ID through one of those fancy contraptions that compiled reports on people's back-grounds, she might as well leave right now.

"It's in my purse, which is in the car. I'm happy to go get it."

"Nice try," he said. "If I march you outside to get it, there's a chance you'll run. If I leave you alone to go look for it myself, you'll leave."

He lifted his phone and started pressing numbers.

"No, don't. Please don't—"

"I'm calling Juliette."

She let out her breath on a sigh. "I thought you were calling 911 again."

He didn't respond. Instead, he pressed the phone to his ear. She must've answered on the first couple of rings.

"Juliette, Ethan Campbell—"

He listened for a moment.

"Sorry to bother you—"

He nodded, opened his mouth to say something and closed it again.

Juliette always had been a talker. It was amusing to watch this tall, gruff, take-charge cowboy be silenced by her. How long would it take before he could get a word in?

If anyone else had been there she'd have wagered with them.

Alas, she was alone and had to enjoy the private audience to this amusing show. When Juliette got back into town, Chelsea fully intended to hug her friend just for being her—and, well, okay, for making

Ethan Campbell stammer as he tried to get a voice-hold in the conversation.

"Juliette—" he said. "Juliette—*Juliette*. Juliette—"

He held the phone away from his ear for a moment and looked up at the ceiling. Chelsea could hear her friend babbling on even though she couldn't tell exactly what she was saying.

Finally, Chelsea did the only thing she could. "Juliette, it's Chelsea!" she called in the loudest voice she could muster. "It's Chelsea *Allen*. Please tell this man you know me and I'm welcome in your home."

Even though Chelsea hadn't been able to understand exactly what Juliette had been talking about a moment ago, she could hear the dramatic silence on the line now and knew Juliette had heard her. She could only pray that Chelsea remembered the *code*.

Chelsea Allen was the name she'd used back in their university days when she wanted to lay low. Rather than unloading her full name, Lady Chelsea Ashford Alden, which always made people change. They treated humble, unassuming Chelsea *Allen* like a regular person. Not like the sister of a famous fashion designer or someone whose brother was likely to be the next prime minister. *Chelsea Allen* was a nobody, and nobody wanted anything from her. Sometimes it was just so much easier to keep things simple. It had been several years since she and Juliette had been out together and she'd played the Chelsea Allen card, but surely Juliette would remember. Of course she would.

Frowning even more pronounced than when he'd

first cornered her, Ethan put the phone back to his ear. "Juliette, do you know a woman named Chelsea Allen?"

Juliette was still talking. Ethan's gaze flicked to Chelsea. As he listened his frown faded to a scowl.

"Yes. She's right here. Standing in your hall bathroom. Yep…Sure…Yeah. Right here in your bathtub, to be exact…No, she's not taking a bath…I caught her coming in through the shower window…It's a long story…No, she's fully clothed…Juliette, listen to me. All I need to know is whether or not she's a friend of yours."

Chelsea couldn't help it. She laughed out loud.

Buggers, she was still in the bathtub. She steadied herself with one hand on the wall and stepped out of the tub onto the black-and-white-tile floor.

A moment later Ethan held out the phone to Chelsea. "Juliette wants to talk to you."

She couldn't resist a smug smile as she took the phone from him.

"Jules? Hi!"

The sound of Juliette's warm laughter emanated across the line. "Chelsea, oh, no! Oh, my gosh. I'm so sorry. I was supposed to leave a key for you. I completely forgot to set it out before I left. Obviously, I forgot to close the bathroom window, too."

"Jules, it's okay. Will you tell Deputy Dawg to stand down, please?"

"You always did know how to make an entrance."

"I know, right? But for future reference, I'd rather use the front door than an open window. Scaling walls isn't my best sport. Please tell Ethan it's okay for me to be here. He's about ready to have me hauled off to jail."

With the phone pressed up to her ear, she brushed past him because she was starting to feel a bit claustrophobic in the bathroom. As she made her exit, her shoulder grazed Ethan's very solid chest. If she hadn't found the guy so annoying, she might've found the sheer masculine bulk of him quite sexy.

"Oh, Ethan's bark is definitely worse than his bite. He's a warm and cuddly teddy bear once you get to know him."

*Warm and cuddly? More like ripped and solid as steel.*

"And you're speaking from experience, I presume?"

Juliette snorted. "Um, *no.* I'll tell you all about him later. For now, give him the phone and I'll tell him you're welcome to be there. Make yourself at home. Help yourself to anything. There's tea in the cupboard by the stove and I just froze the rest of a homemade lasagna. I'll be home tomorrow afternoon. We certainly have a lot to talk about."

Chelsea glanced at Ethan, who was not even trying to pretend he wasn't listening. There was no way she could tell Juliette that escaping from the mess that had become her life was going to be a lot harder than she thought. She'd already been forced into hiding, and on day one of hiding in Celebration, Texas, she'd nearly had a run-in with the authorities.

There was a long pause on the other end of the line

and Chelsea could virtually hear Juliette's wheels turning with unasked questions.

"We certainly do have a lot to talk about. I'll tell you when you get home." She locked gazes with Ethan. "In the meantime, will you please tell the teddy bear I'm welcome to stay?"

Ethan snorted. "Teddy bear?" But she ignored him.

"Thanks, Jules. I appreciate this so much."

Chelsea Allen was hiding something. That much was certain. Ethan didn't know what, but Chelsea had seemed jumpier than a box of bullfrogs on a trampoline.

It went beyond being startled after unexpectedly confronting someone inside a house she'd assumed was empty. His gut was telling him that the woman was hiding something, and his gut was rarely wrong.

But after Chelsea had finished talking to Juliette, she'd handed the phone back to Ethan, and Jules had told him in no uncertain terms that Chelsea was not only welcome at her place, but if she wanted to come and go through the bathroom window, too, that was her prerogative. That was the thing about Juliette Lowell; she was sweet and naive and tended to only see the best in people. That was exactly why Ethan intended to keep an eye on this Chelsea Allen.

At least she was easy on the eyes. It wouldn't be too big of a hardship. But since Juliette had given her blessing for Chelsea to stay, he'd have to continue his neighborly duty from afar.

After he'd hung up the phone, he'd gotten in his

truck, called Joyce back and reported that everything had checked out with Juliette. Then he'd headed to Murphy's Pub. The place he'd been headed to before he'd been waylaid by the strange car in Juliette's driveway. Tonight the Dallas Cowboys were duking it out with the Miami Dolphins and all he wanted to do was belly up to the bar and watch the game.

As he pulled open the pub's front door, he was met by the sound of cheers and hollers. He glanced at the big-screen TV over the bar. The Cowboys had landed a first down, setting up a first and goal situation.

He muttered an oath under his breath because he'd missed the play.

He'd intended to get here in plenty of time to order his dinner—the cheeseburger platter with the works and a nonalcoholic beer—before kickoff, but thanks to Chelsea Allen he had missed nearly the entire first quarter.

Murphy's was crowded tonight, but there were still a few open spaces at the bar. A lot of people had turned out to see the game. On football nights, Murphy's ran specials on beer and their very own signature *Cowboy burger.* Ethan claimed the closest seat and settled in, raising a hand in a quick greeting to Jack Murphy, who was at the helm of the bar.

"Hey, bro," Jack said. "I was wondering where you were tonight. Be right with ya."

Murphy's Pub was one of Celebration's best-loved community gathering spots. It was a casual place and one of Ethan's favorite haunts. It was the kind of place where he could get out and be among people yet not really feel obligated to interact or explain why he was drinking sweet tea or nonalcoholic beer at a bar on a Saturday night rather than imbibing like the rest of the drunken fools.

The long teak bar ran the length of the wall to the left of the entrance. Murphy's bartenders prided themselves on their ability to mix any drink known to mankind, plus several originals that had been invented on the premises and named after local notables.

One quirk of the joint was they were proud of the fact that they only stocked a standard offering of American beers. None of those frou-frou microbrew abominations that seemed to be sprouting like mushrooms everywhere you looked these days. Ask Pop Murphy for something like that and he was likely to direct you to the local cantina Taco's or to a trendy start-up in Dallas.

But it didn't matter to Ethan since he had been sober for two years, three months and one week to the day. All he needed was his favorite brand of nonalcoholic beer, which the Murphys always kept in stock for him.

Even though he couldn't say staying sober today was any easier than it had been the first day he'd made the decision to go cold turkey and turn his life around, each day he stayed out of the bottle and in control of himself was its own victory. He wasn't about to break his winning streak now.

Some who knew of his struggles thought he was crazy to hang out at a place like Murphy's. They thought he was making it extra hard on himself by surrounding himself with the poison.

No. He had a handle on the drinking. Everything was under control. He didn't have to give up going out. He'd worked damn hard to get here and he had no intentions of sliding back into that dark hellhole he'd landed in after his divorce.

He was a recovered alcoholic. That didn't mean he had to be a shut-in, too.

*One day at a time.* The AA slogan had been his mantra when he was going through the hardest times. Now that he was stronger, now that he was sober, he liked to test himself by sitting at Murphy's bar, watching everyone else tip back a few too many. The smell of bourbon might tempt him, but it would never break him. Never.

Jack came back with an open bottle of fake brew and set it down on a napkin in front of him.

"Thanks, man," Ethan said and ordered his dinner.

Jack Murphy wrote it down and walked the ticket over to the kitchen window at the far end of the bar.

"Order," he called to the cook as he hung the green ticket on a clothespin strung at the ready in the order pass-through window between the bar and the kitchen.

Family owned and operated for more than a century, Murphy's was an institution around here. It was one of the oldest businesses in downtown Celebration, and had occupied the same spot since the Murphy brothers had opened their doors in the early 1900s. Not only had it survived prohibition, it had also expanded into abutting spaces over the years and had grown into the place it was today.

As Ethan nursed his drink, he squinted at the television, trying to catch up on what he'd missed of the game. It was still scoreless, but the Cowboys were making good use of their turn and were inching closer to a touchdown. At the very least they should get out of this with a field goal.

At least Chelsea Allen hadn't made him miss anything important. As he took a long draw from the amber bottle, he wondered what she was doing in that house all alone tonight. But before he could swallow, he reminded himself that it wasn't his business. Juliette had said she was welcome. Chelsea and whatever she was hiding wasn't his concern. If he knew what was good for him he'd put her out of his mind.

Juliette was due home tomorrow afternoon. Since Ethan was watching her dog, maybe he'd help her out and take Franklin home and make sure everything was still copacetic, that Chelsea Allen hadn't worn out her welcome.

It was the least a good neighbor could do.

When the TV network took a commercial break, Ethan relaxed. Inhaling the scent of booze, stale beer and fried food, he let his gaze sweep the joint to see who'd come out tonight. As he suspected, it was the regular crowd. Most of them had come to Murphy's to watch the game and grab some dinner like he had.

Some had no interest in sports and danced to the music that played from the jukebox in the adjoining room. Others were crowded around tables, laughing and talking. Another subset, like his friend Aiden Woods, had come out to shoot pool. Looked like Aiden was beating Miles Mercer. Aiden's wife, Bia, the editor-in-chief of the *Dallas Journal of Business and Development*, sat at a nearby table with Miles's wife, Sydney, sipping red wine and sharing animated conversation.

All the other pool tables, which took up a good portion of the front room, were occupied. They always seemed to be in demand. As usual, Murphy's was rocking with a good cross section of people from the Celebration community who kept the place buzzing with good energy.

"Hey, Campbell, I hear you caught the burglar." Zane Phillips slid onto the empty bar stool next to Ethan and ordered a shot of bourbon, neat.

Good news traveled fast around this town. Since Zane had heard, that meant Ethan was going to be the butt of a few good-natured jokes for a while, but he still wasn't sorry for making sure Chelsea was on the up and up.

"Yep." Ethan took another long pull from his drink. "And she was hot."

Zane's right brow shot up. "I guess being the self-appointed neighborhood watch captain has some perks, after all."

These days, everyone in Celebration was a little jumpier since the break-ins had started three months ago. Now neighbors were extra vigilant and took even more care to look out for each other. It was the decent thing to do, even if it meant calling in the occasional false alarm. Better safe than sorry.

"Just being neighborly," Ethan shot back. "I told Jules I'd keep an eye on her place while she's out of town. I saw a strange car in the driveway. I let myself in with the key she gave me and checked it out. No big deal."

"But she was hot, huh? Are you calling dibs?"

Ethan slanted a sideways glance at Zane. *Dibs?* What kind of lame-ass question was that? Besides, Zane had a girlfriend. Granted, the relationship was probably nearing its expiration date. Zane was a serial monogamist. He tended to date one woman at a time, but he never could make a permanent commitment.

When Jack set a platter heaped with a bacon-mushroom cheeseburger and onion rings down in front of Ethan, he trained his focus on his meal.

"So, who is this chick?" Zane asked as Ethan bit into his burger.

He took his time chewing and swallowing. "An old college pal of Juliette's, apparently." Ethan turned his attention to the game on the big screen. He'd come to Murphy's tonight to watch the game, not talk about Juliette's houseguest. "You want to meet her? Go knock on the door."

Zane Phillips was one of his best friends. They'd grown up together and Zane had even stood up for him as best man when he married Molly. He wasn't sure why the thought of the guy getting his grubby paws on Chelsea rubbed him the wrong way. He signaled Jack for another round and hoped Zane got the hint that he didn't feel like talking.

"All kidding aside, it's too bad you didn't catch the bastard," Zane said in a rare moment of sober good sense. "Whoever has been committing these break-ins is still out there. We have to make sure everyone is still on their guard."

Ethan nodded. The Cowboys scored and the place erupted in a cacophony of shouts and cheers.

"On another note, Rachel over at Bistro Saint-Germain said Lucy says she's finally going to open that party barn she's been talking about."

Lucy was his baby sister. Since she'd moved back home from California last year, she'd been threatening to turn the old barn down on the lower forty of their family's farm into an events venue.

Since she seemed to approach life in fits and starts, going gung ho until she lost interest on the project du jour, this idea had become known as the *party barn*.

"Yeah?" Ethan said, taking another bite. He'd stopped expending too much energy on his little sister's whims. It was hard to take her seriously after the fourth or fifth time that she'd jumped into something with both feet, only to move on to the next big thing.

"Sounds like she's serious about this," Zane said. "Maybe the twelfth time's a charm. I told her to invite me to the grand opening party."

Ethan harrumphed. "Don't hold your breath."

He wasn't worried that the party barn might actually become a reality. In all fairness, Lucy wanted to make the place a venue for weddings and other swanky events. She'd latched on to the idea after Juliette's wedding planning business had grown legs and had become a runaway success. Juliette had offhandedly mentioned that the closest wedding venue to Celebration was the Regency Cypress Plantation and Botanical Gardens, which was on the northern edge of Celebration. Lucy swore their grandparents' old barn was an untapped gold mine. Ethan didn't get it. The dilapidated pile of kindling needed to be burned down, not cobbled back together.

It wasn't that he didn't support Lucy. She and their brother, Jude, had inherited some money and equal interest in the family's 900-acre ranch. Since Jude was living the high life on the Professional Bull Riders' circuit, he and Lucy had left Ethan with the task of reviving Triple C's once floundering horse-breeding business. Ethan had worked hard to turn it around and breathe new life into it. Since the breeding arm of Triple C was all his doing, the siblings had mutually decided to divvy up the land, each claiming a specific 300-acre area. Ethan got the land with the stables and the home where they'd grown up. Lucy had chosen the plot with their grandparents' old house and the barn. Jude's was untouched acreage.

Lucy could do whatever she wanted with her piece of land. She was perfectly within her rights to turn it into an events venue. Hell, she could turn it into a zoo if she wanted. It was her call. However, over the past three years she'd had the attention span of a fruit fly. She'd already blown through every cent of the money she'd inherited after their parents died and she'd maxed out her credit cards and was left with the debt.

Ethan had helped her out financially until she could find a job with a steady paycheck that allowed her to start paying off her cards. As far as Ethan knew, she was still paying. Now that she was supporting herself, he wasn't going to enable another whim. When she'd asked Ethan to cosign for a loan so she could have some party barn start-up money, he'd declined.

If he was completely honest, his refusal wasn't just tough love. Ethan had often worried that his siblings might have the same alcoholic gene that had almost gotten the best of him. It ran in their family. In fact, it had cost their father his life. Their dad had been sauced the night of the car crash that had killed him. For a while it had been touch and go for their mother, who had landed in the ICU.

She'd lived, but she'd come out of the accident a paraplegic because of damage to one of the lower thoracic nerves. She passed away about a year later.

The disease hadn't hooked its claws into Jude, who seemed to have his act together—even if he never did come home. Ethan still worried about Lucy. She was only twenty-five. She had done some things in the past—like getting caught drunk skinny-dipping in the pond out back of old man Jenkins's hunting lodge—that made him question whether or not she was immune to alcohol's hereditary choke hold.

For some ridiculous reason completely out of left field, Ethan found himself wondering if Chelsea

Allen, the woman who'd already proven herself capable of breaking into houses, had ever been skinny-dipping.

As he chased away the inappropriate image with a sip of his beer, for a split second he craved a shot of something a hell of a lot stronger than nonalcoholic beer.

After Ethan's own hard-traversed path to sobriety, he worried that being in a party environment—even if it would be mostly wedding receptions—wouldn't be good for Lucy.

Sure, she was a grown woman, but she would always be his little sister. She and Jude were all the family he had left. His stance against the party barn stemmed from simply wanting to protect her. Jude may have been the prodigal brother, but Ethan was the protector. As any good big brother would, he wanted to hold back the tide and keep it from drowning her.

Even if the jury was still out on whether or not she was susceptible to the alcoholic gene, her previous, half-baked business ventures indicated she might not possess entrepreneurial instincts, either.

Obviously, she'd been talking about the party barn enough that word was starting to get around town. She hadn't mentioned any more about it to him. But really, was that so hard to believe? Sometimes he felt like he was the last to know anything. Such as how he'd had no idea that Juliette had such a beautiful friend. Whether or not that friend was hiding something or hiding *from* something, Ethan couldn't deny that she'd been front and center in his brain all night.

He hadn't had this kind of reaction to a pretty woman in a very long time.

He'd definitely stop by Juliette's tomorrow and see what Chelsea Allen was up to.

## Chapter Three

The next morning when Chelsea's eyes fluttered open, it took her a moment to remember that she was safe in the sanctuary of Juliette's spare bedroom, where there was enough floral damask to rival Queen Mary's gardens at the Regent's Park. There were roses everywhere: on the duvet, the curtains, the wingback chair and tufted ottoman. It was so Juliette and it warmed Chelsea from the inside out.

She luxuriated in a long, slow, full-body stretch and then squinted at the clock on the nightstand to check the time. It was after nine o'clock. She should get up and get a wiggle on. Really, she should, she thought as she sank deeper into the warm bed.

Her body and mind had needed the rest. It dawned on her that this was the first time she'd slept through the night without waking since her life had blown up in the press last week, when she'd been humiliated and reduced to being the subject of lewd jokes and perverted voyeurism. Her ex-boyfriend had recorded them without her permission and released the footage, yet she was the villain. Her siblings couldn't look her in the eyes. Her parents didn't even want to see her face, much less help her solve the problem. They had made it perfectly clear that it was her problem. She needed to make it go away—or at least go away until it had passed.

Recently, it had been the last thing she'd thought about before she went to sleep and the first thing on her mind when she'd awoken. Until today.

This morning the first thought that had crossed her mind was flowers.

She felt safe here. Not that the press couldn't find her in Celebration, Texas. But with neighbors looking out for neighbors and scaring away those who didn't belong the way Ethan Campbell had last night, it would certainly make it more difficult for anyone to sneak up on her the way the reporters had in London.

Chelsea pressed the heels of her hands into her eyes, determined to exorcise the media demons. She drew in a measured deep breath, held it for a few beats and exhaled.

Visions of the reporters went away, but thoughts of Ethan Campbell remained.

In the light of day he didn't annoy her as much as he had last night. Of course, she was rested this morning and that made the whole world look better.

She took another healing breath and reminded herself everything would be okay.

Eventually.

She would put her life back together and maybe even look back at this time and laugh. Well, perhaps not laugh. That was pushing it, but she was resilient and she would be fine soon enough.

In the meantime, she had a lovely place to stay and the company of a good friend with whom she looked forward to catching up.

She'd have to figure out how to be helpful and not get under foot. She and Jules had roomed well together at university because they understood each other's quirks and idiosyncrasies. She knew Juliette well enough that she was confident she would be able to size up how her friend felt about Chelsea's invasion the moment she walked through the front door.

Chelsea would not outstay her welcome—though deep down she hoped Juliette would be just as happy to see her as Chelsea was to reconnect with her.

But she was getting ahead of herself. First, tea. Before that could happen, she must get up and put the kettle on. She swung her legs over the side of the bed, stood and pulled on her fuchsia yoga pants.

After Ethan had grudgingly growled off and left her alone last night, Chelsea had made a mad dash outside to get her handbag and suitcase out of the car. She'd managed to make it back inside without drawing any more attention to herself. Or, who knows, maybe Ethan had informed the town that Jules was cool with her being there. She hoped he hadn't told too many people. Juliette had lamented before that people in her hometown could be rather nosy. Some considered it close-knit and neighborly. But Jules had confessed that sometimes, despite good intentions, having the entire town in your business felt a little stifling. As Chelsea drew water and set the kettle on the stove, she hoped they wouldn't be in *her* business—or, more aptly, in Chelsea Allen's.

As she waited for the water to boil, she had a nose around Juliette's cottage. It was cozy and neat as a pin. A mix of old-world charm with modern accents, it was as posh and unique as Juliette herself.

The overstuffed sofa was piled with throw pillows in luscious jewel tones and rich floral patterns. The rough-hewn parquet floor was laid in a herringbone pattern that looked as if it had been lifted from a Belle Époque Paris apartment. The walls were painted a warm, welcoming shade of pale blue, which set off the white crown molding that hugged the tiptops of the home's tall walls. An antique Persian rug anchored the room and presented an interesting contrast to the modern wood-and-glass coffee table.

Chelsea had studied interior design at university and had even done a short stint at a high-end London firm. She loved what Juliette had done with the place. It was as spot-on as any project Chelsea might've planned.

She picked up a small obsidian elephant from an end table and traced a finger over its smooth, curved surface. She'd brought it back from Africa for Juliette.

A year out of university, she'd landed a great job

with a design firm, but then she'd learned about the international aid organization Voluntary Service Overseas and its world aid efforts.

She'd grown up so privileged it seemed the perfect way to give back. Everyone thought she was crazy when she made the decision to leave her design job, which her sister, Victoria, had helped her land, in favor of shipping off to Africa.

Despite the rolled eyes and reproach she'd received from her family and their accusations that she refused to grow up—and this sojourn was just an excuse to put off true responsibility—she maxed out her time in Africa helping to further the organization's poverty-ending efforts.

She'd been changed by her experience.

When the cost of a frivolous designer throw pillow could feed a starving family for a month, decorating the homes of the überwealthy seemed wrong on so many levels. After she aged out of VSO, Chelsea couldn't bring herself to go back into the design business. Instead, she took a job with the non-profit End Hunger London, which garnered more familial huffs and eye rolls because it wasn't one of their chosen charities. However, because of her family's connections, she was able to draw a respectable amount of recognition and support to the organization.

Even though she never sought personal attention, for a short while, the press deemed her an angel. Until they grew bored with that and they decided to turn her into the devil.

The minor tabloid attention had actually worked

in her favor for a while. After she'd helped get End Hunger London up and rolling, she was ready for a change. The prestigious London firm Hargraves Designs had courted her and hired her as a designer. It was the time for a change. She'd worked for the greater good—and would continue to volunteer and use her high-profile status to raise awareness. It just seemed like the right move. But everything fell apart after Hadden's revenge.

Hargraves wanted edgy, not skanky. They'd let her go, without even giving her a chance to defend herself.

Determined not to turn loose of her good mood, Chelsea returned the elephant to its place and pushed the memories from her mind. She spied several other things that Juliette had purchased when the two of them had traveled together during school—a hand-blown vase from Murano, a beautiful mirror made from vintage plates by Austrian designer Christine Hechinger. The memories made her smile.

But the thing Chelsea found the most endearing, and the most interesting by far, was the plethora of pictures her dear friend had scattered about the place in frames on the walls and on easels as centerpieces of shelf and tabletop arrangements.

Chelsea didn't have to look hard to find several pictures of herself with Juliette. But she couldn't locate a single photograph of Jules with Ethan Campbell. Not that she was looking—or at least she hadn't realized she was looking until it registered that she found his photographic absence strangely satisfying.

On the phone, Jules had denied anything but a platonic, neighborly friendship with Ethan, but they'd only spoken about him for a moment. Then again, Juliette certainly wouldn't have used that opportunity to regale Chelsea with details of a friends-with-benefits arrangement with her hunky neighbor. Not with Ethan standing right there.

Actually, it might've been better if she knew that Juliette *had* hooked up with Ethan, even casually— especially casually—because according to *the friendship code* that would make Ethan off-limits.

And how ridiculous was that thought? But wait… wasn't that guy, that professional bull rider that Juliette had a thing for, named Campbell, too? John… No… Was it Jude? Jude Campbell. Yes. That was it. She hadn't heard Jules mention him in ages. She made a mental note to ask about the connection when Juliette got home.

In the meantime, Chelsea didn't dwell on either of the Campbell men as she soaked in the rest of her best friend's home, focusing on what a treat it was to be there at last.

Though Juliette was born and bred in Celebration, the United Kingdom had always held a special place in her heart. Chelsea used to tease her about being an anglophile because she had loved everything British. Jules had, of course, returned to Celebration, and that was where she had started her business, but her friend had infused enough of England into her Texas home that she had taken the culture with her. The best of both worlds, Chelsea mused as she lifted a frame containing a photo of a corgi puppy. Ahh, this must be Franklin. Juliette had been so excited when she'd texted with the news that she was adopting a puppy from a litter of a corgi that belonged to a local friend.

She was eager to meet the little guy. Since Jules was away, someone must've been watching him. Too bad she couldn't go pick him up and have him here when Jules got home. She'd do just that if she knew where he was, but she didn't. And she didn't want to call Juliette and risk interrupting her at work. But she could text her, and Jules could answer at her convenience. After a momentary hesitation about whether or not it was smart to venture out, she made up her mind that while she would mostly keep a low profile, she had no intentions of sequestering herself while she was here. Nothing said sketchy like a guest who holed up in the house. Plus, she wanted to see where her friend lived.

When they were at university together, Chelsea had wanted to visit Juliette's hometown—she used to joke that she wanted to meet a real cowboy—but Juliette had always steered away from spending their holidays here and they had opted for more exotic locales such as Paris, Milan and Ibiza. After they graduated, though they'd taken care to keep in touch, they both had gotten so bogged down with life after university—Chelsea going to Africa and Jules putting all her time and resources behind her wedding planning business—that they hadn't seen each other in person in three years. If there was one upside to this scandal pushing her away from London, it was this chance to reunite with her best friend.

She sent the text and the kettle whistled. Chelsea returned to the kitchen, turning off the burner. She opted for the Taylors of Harrogate Yorkshire Gold from the selection of fine loose tea in Juliette's cabinet and spooned two teaspoons of the leaves into the mesh strainer, set it in the cup and poured steaming water over the top.

Her tea hadn't even had time to steep properly before Chelsea heard keys rattling in the front door.

*What in the world?*

She wasn't expecting Juliette until this afternoon— possibly even early evening. If Ethan was back, letting himself in without even the common courtesy of a knock, she would have several choice words for him. He might have a key, but that didn't mean he was free to use it and enter at whim while she was here alone.

She left her tea on the kitchen's marble-topped counter and walked into the living room, steeling herself to make it clear she wasn't pleased. She'd had it up to here with guys who thought they could push their way in and—

"Chelsea!" Juliette stepped into the living room, leaving the door wide open as she rushed toward her friend. "You're here! You're really here. I'm so happy to see you."

For the tiniest fraction of a second something that resembled disappointment zinged through Chelsea. But it wasn't disappointment. How could she be disappointed that Jules was here and she wasn't going to get the chance to tell off Ethan Campbell when the last thing she wanted was him barging in?

And she was elated to see Juliette, whom she was so busy enfolding in a warm hug that Ethan Campbell completely left her mind.

*Well, maybe not completely.*

"It's about time you got here," Chelsea said, holding Juliette at arm's length to look at her. "You're just as gorgeous as ever."

And she was. With her perpetually tanned olive skin, long, dark hair and sky blue eyes, she had always been an exotic beauty. Only now she seemed more...grounded. More sure of herself. And why not, with her business booming?

"I left early so I could get back as fast as I could. Now that you're here I may never let you leave. But what's going on? What the hell has Hadden Hastings done now? You know I never liked him."

Why wasn't she prepared for this? She knew she was going to have to tell Juliette the whole story. But she struggled to find the words.

"You must be exhausted," Chelsea said. "Why don't you kick off your shoes? I just boiled some water. While you're getting comfortable, I'll make you a cup of tea."

"That sounds heavenly." Juliette gave Chelsea another quick hug before she disappeared down the hall. "But I want to hear everything. Every last detail."

That was what she was afraid of.

When Juliette returned, she'd traded in her business suit for a soft-looking pink tracksuit.

"You were in San Antonio?" Chelsea asked, hoping to distract her by changing the subject.

Juliette nodded as she plated a couple of muffins and set them and the two mugs of tea on a wooden tray.

"It was a gorgeous wedding. The daughter of a big family that made a fortune in the spice trade."

"The spice trade? What is this, the fifteenth century?"

"Believe it or not, I think that's when they started the company." The two went into the living room and settled themselves on the couch. "But enough about them. What's going on?" Juliette sipped her tea. "Is your mother being impossible again?"

"I wish it were that simple." Chelsea ducked her head. "So I take it you haven't heard?"

"What's going on?" Concern overtook Juliette's face. "You said something about a video Hadden sent to the media. Is everything okay?"

As hot tears began to burn her eyes, Chelsea shook her head. She tried to console herself with the thought that if Juliette hadn't heard about the scandal, maybe it hadn't made its way across the pond.

Juliette reached out and put a hand on Chelsea's arm. "Honey, talk to me. Tell me what's wrong."

"Hadden's quite proud of himself, I'm sure."

Chelsea drew in a deep breath. She just needed to say it. It was like jumping off the high dive; if she thought about it too long she would paralyze herself.

"Before Hadden and I broke up, he filmed us having sex. Once word got out that Thomas might be a contender for prime minister, Hadden gave the tape to the media."

Juliette nearly snorted her tea and was overcome by a coughing fit. When she finally regained her composure, she said, "Are you kidding me?"

Chelsea shook her head. She couldn't force words around the lump of shame that always swelled in her throat when she tried to talk about this.

"That little turd. You could sue him. You could sue him and the media that released it. They didn't have your permission."

"No, they didn't have my permission. I would've never allowed it. I would've never allowed Hadden to record us if I had known. The problem is, I don't have solid proof that Hadden was the one who released the footage. Obviously, you and I both know it couldn't have been anybody but him. There was no one else in his flat while we were intimate—"

Her voice broke and she stared at her hands in her lap. She was so ashamed. Even telling her best friend in the world made her feel as vulnerable and dirty and humiliated as the moment she first found out.

"How dare he?" Juliette railed. "It's called slut-shaming, you know? God, I hate that term. It doesn't do the female gender any favors. Even though it's not intended to be derogatory toward women, it sounds like it is. It is a misnomer. It should be sex-shaming. Please know I am not by any means calling you a slut. You're not. You're the victim here. Don't you see that? This is the epitome of double standards."

"I appreciate your support. I feel pretty crummy

right now. I feel shameful and dirty, but I will never allow Hadden to force me to play the victim. You know me better than that. However, my family thinks *they* are the victims. They want me to disappear, just go away—" she made a shooing motion with her hand "—until this whole ugly mess blows over. I am officially a liability to Thomas's future. So I have been cordially invited to get lost. Thank you for taking me in. I couldn't think of anywhere else I wanted to go."

Juliette threw her arms around Chelsea and enveloped her in another of her famous bear hugs. "I am so glad you're here, honey. Though I wish it were under different circumstances. This isn't your fault, Chels. Hadden is a misogynistic pig. He's a creep. Why is he getting no flack and you're taking all the heat? Why are we not prosecuting him?"

"Because he blurred out his face in the footage. No one can prove it's him."

"And the fact that you dated him for over a year never entered into the tawdry equation?"

"Of course people have speculated, but there's no proof."

Her face burned and she buried it in her hands. Juliette reached out and rubbed her back.

"I am just incensed about this. I mean, I know you would never willingly open your bedroom door. It's such a violation of privacy. But here's one thing I don't get. Why is it still so shameful for a woman to embrace her sexuality, but a man gets points for dipping his wick?"

"That's the age-old dilemma," Chelsea mused.

"One would hope that by now we'd evolved beyond that pathetic double standard. But times like this prove it's alive and well because everyone has branded me a slut and seems to be taking great pleasure in shaming me."

"But you are not a slut! I know the tabloids went to town on you a few years ago when you worked for End Hunger. They tried to turn you into the poster child for party girls. What was that creep's name who kept hounding you?"

"Bertie Veal. He's still up to his antics. He's the one who broke the news about the tape. I just hope he doesn't get wind that I'm here. If he does, I'll have to leave because I don't want him to start bothering you. Let's hope he doesn't remember we were university roommates."

"Bertie doesn't remember me. I was never on his radar. But he was pretty obsessed with you. Actually, I think he had a crush on you, but he knew you were out of his league. It's like the playground bully who pulls a girl's ponytail when she won't pay attention to him. Bertie needs to get a life."

"Sadly, selling stories to the paparazzi *is* his life. After Hadden sold him the tape of us, Bertie has been insufferable."

"But you really haven't done anything more than the average twentysomething. Your father just happens to be the Earl of Downing and your brother might be prime minister. That makes you a prime target. An interesting target."

Juliette shrugged as if it was no big deal.

Chelsea knew Juliette meant well. But she wished she could tell her friend this wasn't making her feel any better. Similar arguments had been bandied about beyond the tabloids and in the conventional news media. All it managed to accomplish was to draw more attention to the fact that pictures and videos were at the fingertips of anyone who cared to call them up on the internet and watch the peep show. She'd come to Celebration to get away from this. Not to dwell on it.

"Yet, I'm sure Hadden is getting high fives and slaps on the back for being such a big man. Can't they find out the original IP address of the person who leaked it? I mean, your brother is a member of parliament. He knows the queen, for God's sake. Can't he get the Secret Intelligence Service on it? You do have an attorney at least, don't you?"

Chelsea buried her face in her hands for a moment before answering.

"Thomas helped me retain an attorney and he has an old school chum who is working on getting the video removed from the internet. My brother is doing what he can, but he's walking a fine line. The problem is, the video is like a virus. It's removed from one site and it pops up on three more."

"Oh, honey, I'm sorry."

Her father was more concerned that Hadden's vendetta might derail Thomas's shot at being prime minister should his party come to power than he was that his daughter's privacy and dignity had been violated. As far as her parents were concerned, this entire ordeal was her fault. If she'd been more rooted, more focused on something constructive rather than floating about trying to find herself, Hadden would've never had the opportunity; this disgrace would've never happened.

"The point of the scandal was to get back at me by bringing down Thomas and making him look bad during this time when every eye in the UK is on him. I just—" Chelsea felt tears brimming again, and she covered her face with her hands. "I can't, Jules. I just can't do this right now."

Juliette set down her tea, got to her feet in a flash and put her arms around Chelsea. "I'm so sorry. That was insensitive of me. I didn't mean to make you feel bad. This is not your fault. Your privacy was violated in the worst way possible. I can't stand the fact that that smug asshat Hadden Hastings is walking around with his head held high while people and the press are treating you like it's the puritanical seventeenth century and you should have a big red *A* pinned to the front of you."

Maybe it was because her emotions were running high, maybe it was because she was so tired of feeling so small and dirty, but something about the far-fetched *Scarlet Letter* reference struck her as funny.

"If you're likening me to Hester Prynne, I'm not married, and thank God I didn't get pregnant with Hadden's child." But saying the facts out loud didn't sound as humorous as they'd sounded in her head. "Look, I appreciate you taking my side, but can we

please change the subject to something more interesting?"

As Juliette nodded, she still looked as if she was
spoiling for a fight with Hadden.

"I've been dying to know whether or not your
neighbor Ethan Campbell is related to your old boyfriend, Jude Campbell. He is. Am I right?"

Juliette grimaced and Chelsea was surprised when
her eyes darkened even more. "Yes. They're brothers.
But I haven't seen Jude since I moved back to Celebration after college. He's been away living large on
the Professional Bull Riding circuit. As far as I'm
concerned, he can stay away."

"You're still nursing the Jude wound?"

Juliette chewed her bottom lip instead of answering.

"Well, Ethan seems pretty attentive," Chelsea said.

"Yeah, he's a great guy. He and his brother are as
different as night and day."

"So, are you interested in Ethan? I mean, come on,
Ethan is pretty darn hot, even if he is a little uptight.
You could do a lot worse."

"Ethan is like a big brother. He's just a good guy
who looks out for me."

"*Looks out* for you, huh? I think he has his eye
on you."

Juliette flinched. "Ethan? No. Not a chance." Her
mouth flattened into a distasteful straight line and
she shook her head. She might have made the same
face if Chelsea had asked her to eat the soggy loose
leaves from the dregs at the bottom of the teapot. "He

is not my type. There's definitely nothing happening in that arena."

And there it was, the companion to the strange satisfaction she'd felt earlier when she'd looked for Ethan's picture among Juliette's home gallery and didn't find it.

"I mean his brother Jude and I were pretty serious for a long time."

"Do you ever hear from him?"

"Nope, and I'd rather not talk about him." Her smile seemed a bit forced and her nod a little too resolute.

"All right, but you know I'm here if you ever do want to talk." Juliette nodded and Chelsea knew it was time to change the subject. "Thank you for letting me stay with you, Jules. I won't impose too long. If it gets to be too much having me under foot, I can find a place to stay in town."

Juliette put her hands on her hips. "You can stay with me as long as you like. I'm so happy you're here."

Chelsea grimaced. "You might not want to give me an open-ended invitation. Because I just might take you up on it."

"Maybe you should."

Sweet, generous Juliette. The thought about house-guests and fish came to mind, and even though she didn't want to argue it right now, she knew she *should* find alternate lodging as soon as she got her bearings.

"It's such a lovely day," Juliette said. "Let's take

our tea outside to the patio. I think we could both use some fresh air."

Chelsea followed her outside. The backyard looked transformed in the light of day. Her gaze skittered to the bathroom window she'd used to gain entrance last night and she found herself reliving the start she'd felt when she saw Ethan Campbell's muscled frame blocking the doorway. The chair she'd used to boost herself up was still turned over on its side, exactly where it had fallen the night before.

Chelsea walked over and picked it up, returning it to the patio table where she'd found it.

"Part of the crime scene from last night," she said sheepishly.

"I see," Juliette said. "I'm so sorry the key wasn't under the mat like I said it would be. We've had some break-ins around here. I'd taken it inside and I was in such a rush to get to this job, it completely slipped my mind to put it outside again like I promised."

The two of them settled themselves at the table and each reclaimed her mug of tea.

"It's not a problem." Chelsea smiled. "If there has been crime in the area, you shouldn't leave the key outside. Not even for one night. And you probably shouldn't leave the bathroom window open, for that matter."

They sipped in companionable silence for a few moments.

"So, is your gorgeous neighbor married?" Chelsea heard herself asking before she could think better of it.

"Why? Are *you* interested?"

"Absolutely not," she snapped. "I'm just curious."

Okay, well, under a different set of circumstances she might be. She tended to have a thing for tall, dark-haired guys with blue eyes and mile-wide shoulders. But now was not the time to indulge such fancies. "I'm here to disappear, not to land myself in deeper trouble. The even more pressing matter is to find myself a place to stay."

Though maybe a temporary fling with a handsome cowboy would be a good way to keep her mind off her troubles. She'd just have to be careful. Make sure it was on her terms.

"You're staying here," Juliette said. "End of discussion, okay?"

"You're too good to me," Chelsea said.

"It's the least I can do. How many times over the years did I stay with your family?"

Chelsea snorted. "Trust me. Your presence never inconvenienced them because they were never at home."

Chelsea's gaze scanned the backyard, which she realized was actually a beautiful, well-tended English garden in full bloom. Juliette always had loved her flowers. Especially English gardens.

"At least when you stayed with me at Longbridge Hall you never caused a commotion like I did last night," Chelsea said. "And you must've gotten up at the crack of dawn to make it back so early. See, I'm already being *that* guest."

"I was on the road by six, but you gave me an excuse to get out of there."

"Better you than me." Chelsea chuckled and raised her mug to her friend. "This is my first cup of tea."

Juliette laughed. "You've never been a morning person, have you?"

Chelsea gave a *you're-right*, one-shoulder shrug and sipped her tea.

"Look, I know my place isn't fancy, but—"

Chelsea held up a hand and stopped her. "Don't be ridiculous. Your home is lovely. I'd choose it any day over Longbridge Hall. But really, Jules, you don't need a long-term houseguest skulking about when you get home from a job."

"I'm not going to argue about this. You could never be a mere *houseguest*." Juliette reached out and put a hand on Chelsea's arm. "You're the sister I've always wanted."

"A sister who's toting a lot of baggage these days." Chelsea's cheeks warmed and she dropped her gaze to her teacup. Would this humiliation ever fade? This was Jules, after all.

The timing couldn't have been worse given Thomas's prime minister candidacy, but maybe this was the boot to the seat she'd needed to start getting her act together.

Chelsea heard the sound of a car door shutting and a dog barking.

"That sounds like Franklin," Juliette said, pushing away from the table and standing. "Ethan must've brought him home."

*"Ethan?"* Dear God in heaven, did all roads in

this town lead to Ethan Campbell? She ignored the thought that hoped so.

"Yes, he watches my dog when I go out of town."

"He seems to be a neighborly kind of guy, doesn't he?" Chelsea said, mostly to herself.

As they rounded the house, they saw Ethan standing on the front porch, knocking on the door.

"Hey, neighbor," Juliette said, casting a sidelong glance at Chelsea as she bent to love on her little dog. "We were just talking about you."

"You were?"

But Juliette was too busy cooing words of adoration and praise to her wiggling four-legged love to answer Ethan, whose gaze had locked with Chelsea's. He nodded his greeting and she felt her cheeks warm.

"Hello," she said, careful to keep her accent in check.

"Yes, I was just telling Chelsea that you're so good to look out for Franklin and me while I'm away. You didn't have to bring him home. I was coming over later, anyway."

"You were?" Ethan asked.

"Yes." She gave Franklin a hand signal and he followed her onto the porch. "This afternoon I'm looking at the barn with Lucy. Didn't she tell you?"

*Who was Lucy? Ahh, his girlfriend, probably.*

Made sense. Guys like Ethan Campbell usually had a girlfriend—or a wife.

A voice inside her reminded her that she knew nothing about Ethan Campbell beyond his being the eyes and ears of the neighborhood watch team.

And the fact that he was tall and muscled and good-looking as sin. But good-looking guys were the root of all the trouble she was in now.

Good-looking guys…guys who were tall and had broad shoulders were her Achilles' heel. She needed to stop being so shallow, stop allowing herself to be wooed by the promise of washboard abs. Because judging by the way his body went from broad shoulders to a strong, broad chest and veed perfectly into slim cowboy hips, she'd just bet there was a six-pack hiding out under that chambray work shirt.

She really should strive to be a better person and look beyond the physical…beyond the deliciousness of blue eyes and curly brown hair and focus on more important attributes—like the way Ethan's biceps had bunched and muscled as he held open the screen door and gestured for Chelsea to enter first.

*All that and good manners, too.*

"No, Lucy did not tell me you were coming over to look at the barn," he said, that familiar irritation he'd displayed last night coating his words today. "I hear she's starting up with that nonsense again. Juliette, don't encourage her."

He closed the screen door behind him, keeping his hand on it so that it didn't slam. Score another point for the cowboy with manners.

"Ethan Campbell, why wouldn't you want your sister to do something that made her happy?"

*Sister?*

Lucy was his *sister*?

*Well, then. Score one—a big one—for Chelsea.*

She bent down to stroke Franklin's velvety-soft ears and to hide her grin. "Nice, Franklin," she cooed. "It's good to meet you."

She focused on the dog's little corgi smile and the eraser-pink tongue that lolled to one side of his mouth, giving him an affable look. She'd always thought the corgi breed, with their happy personalities and short, stubby little legs, were the *court jesters* of all dogs. They made people happy just by being in the same room. That was why she was smiling, not because Lucy was Ethan's sister.

"I do want my sister to be happy," he said.

She wasn't smiling at the way his biceps were flexing again as he braced his hand against the doorjamb or at the way his eyes crinkled at the corners when he looked concerned.

"You know her track record when it comes to seeing things through to the end. She has a tendency to abandon projects when she loses interest. She doesn't need to waste any more money. She's still paying off debt from that fabric business she left school to start."

Juliette sighed. "I get that this is a big endeavor. It's huge. But now that my business is booming, I'm in a position to send a lot of my business her way."

Ethan must've noticed Chelsea's puzzled expression. "My sister wants to turn an old barn on the outer edge of our property into a party barn."

He gave his head a quick shake like it was the dumbest idea he'd ever heard.

"Not a *party barn*," Juliette corrected. "It's an events venue. There's nothing like it for miles around here. It's a completely untapped market and a great idea that she needs to take advantage of before someone else does. Barn weddings are all the rage right now."

Franklin walked over to his mistress, sat down and leaned against her leg as if showing his support.

"I seriously doubt many people would want to get married in a barn, out here in the middle of nowhere. The place is falling down. It's more of a shanty than a barn."

"That's why we need to renovate it," Juliette said.

"What's that going to cost?" Ethan crossed his arms in front of him. There were those biceps again, beckoning her from under his long-sleeve shirt.

*Hello there, lovelies.*

"Chelsea is a designer," Juliette said. "She might be able to give us an idea of the scope involved, and she and I can help Lucy bid out the work."

Chelsea blinked. "Oh. What?"

"The work on the barn. You have to see it, Chels. It has so much potential."

"I'm not licensed," she said. "Not here."

"Well, you have a design degree. You wouldn't be doing the work. Just rendering an opinion. Helping Ethan see the place's potential."

Ethan was frowning at her as if she couldn't convince him that the crown jewels had worth, but Juliette was nodding and looking so hopeful.

"Chelsea doesn't want to get involved." Ethan was talking to Juliette, but he was still looking at Chelsea.

"I don't mind giving it a look-see and offering my

opinion." Chelsea raised her chin, a defense under his scrutiny. "That's not exactly getting involved, is it now?"

"So y'all are going to gang up on me." Ethan laughed—a humorless sound—and shook his head. "I'll definitely be there for the walk-through, then. Because I'm not about to turn you all loose at Lucy's whim." He pinned his gaze on Chelsea. "Especially if *you're* going to be there. I knew you were trouble the minute I laid eyes on you."

She might have found his words offensive if not for the mischievous sparkle in his eyes that was more of a sexy challenge than an accusation. It made her breath catch before it sent her stomach into a rushing spiral.

*Trouble? Oh, Cowboy, you have no idea.*

## Chapter Four

"Basically, you're working with a blank canvas," Chelsea said. Ethan watched her turn around and survey the interior of the old weathered barn. "Anything is possible."

Anything? If they asked him, he'd say it would be easier to burn the damn thing down and start from scratch.

With its dirt floor and wood rot that let daylight in through the cracks—*blank canvas* wasn't how he would've described the place, but they hadn't asked him. Chelsea was the expert.

The woman was full of surprises and apparently full of hope for this godforsaken place.

Or maybe she was just trying to be polite and not dash Lucy's dreams.

Pretty *and* polite.

That was a lethal combination.

Last night he hadn't thought *polite* was one of her attributes. But then again, last night he probably hadn't made the best first impression, either. He'd been gruff and she'd been feistier than an old barn cat that had been cornered by a skunk.

*Polite* hadn't exactly been on the table last night.

Today was a completely different story. She was freshly scrubbed and makeup-free. Her long, blond hair was pulled back in a ponytail, accentuating high cheekbones and a bottom lip that was slightly fuller than the top, giving her a look of near innocence. Near, but not quite.

She wore a simple blue T-shirt that brought out the color of her eyes and hugged her curves in all the right places. The woman standing in front of him this morning looked like a different person from the one he'd nearly had arrested last night.

Ethan had to make a concentrated effort not to stare at her. It helped when he reminded himself that Ms. Polite and Pretty was in cahoots with Juliette, and the two of them were filling Lucy's head with all kinds of dangerous ideas that would probably cost a fortune.

This initial consultation might be free, but he worried about the pretty picture Chelsea would paint as she convinced Lucy that she just couldn't live without all the bells and whistles a designer could provide at a steep markup. Wasn't that what designers did? Especially ones who entered a house through the bathroom window and managed to sweet-talk him out of turning her over to the sheriff.

"So you're saying we can do anything we want?" Lucy's eyes lit up.

"Whatever your budget will allow," Chelsea qualified.

Ethan braced himself. How much was that *budget* going to set his sister back? He had to be the voice of reason. "*Budget* is the key word, Lucy. Maybe you should finish paying off your debt and save some money before you jump into this."

His sister ignored him.

The only thing of value Lucy had left was this property. She didn't have any money. She'd spent the small amount of cash she'd inherited on her stint in graphic design school in New York and her subsequent move to California where she'd leaped right into a bad business deal. A friend she'd met in design school had talked her into moving out West where they'd endeavored to design their own line of fabrics. Ethan had warned her to do some due diligence before she rushed headlong into the partnership, but Lucy swore she knew what she was doing, that she had everything under control. Even though he'd seen the train wreck coming from a mile away, Ethan was fool enough to leave her to her own devices. Because, of course, Lucy was a grown woman. Even if she was his little sister, she was old enough to make her own decisions and suffer the consequences of her actions.

It was true. He knew it. But it didn't make it any

easier to watch his sister setting herself up to crash and burn again.

A party barn? Out here in the middle of nowhere?

People got married in churches or hotels or parks, not in gussied-up barns out in the middle of an overgrown field.

But what did he know? Juliette and Chelsea seemed to think it was the best idea since the invention of the telephone. And he did trust Juliette.

His sister had always been attached to this ramshackle pile of kindling that they called a barn. Always had been, ever since their grandparents had lived in the bungalow next door.

They'd been gone for nearly fifteen years and Lucy had moved into their house when she'd returned from California last fall.

While he knew the house and the land meant too much to her to sell, if she mortgaged the house to secure a loan she could inadvertently lose it all if she made another bad business decision. Lucy was headstrong and sometimes she latched onto ideas like this the way a pit bull grabbed hold of a soup bone. There was no reasoning with her, no loosening her grip on anything once it took root.

He had the sinking feeling thanks to the pretty picture Chelsea had just painted, he might be too late to talk some sense into her.

"Could we add on a second story, so while a wedding was going on down here, the caterer could be upstairs getting everything ready for the reception?" Lucy asked. "After the ceremony, the guests could walk right up to the reception. Ooh! Or you know what would be cool? What if we had two areas upstairs? One area where the guests could have hors d'oeuvres and cocktails, and another part we could keep separate where the dinner and dancing would take place once the bride and groom were done with photos. Could we do that?"

*Cha-ching.*

"Actually, that's a great idea," Juliette said. "In other barn venues we've had to hold the ceremony outside so the caterer could set up the reception inside the barn. If it rains, it creates big problems. So if a second story is feasible, it would solve a lot of problems. At least the bride would have peace of mind that the weather wouldn't wreck her day. Can we do it?"

All eyes turned to Chelsea. "As I said, it depends on your budget." She glanced at Ethan and seemed to weigh her words. Maybe she was taking what he'd said to heart. "But sure. The ceiling is high enough that it could work. Do you have a contractor?"

"Sounds expensive," Ethan preempted with his reality check before Lucy could get even more attached to the idea.

But he was too late. "I don't care if it's expensive," Lucy said. "Anything worth doing is worth doing right."

"Where are you going to get the money?" he asked.

His sister waved him off with a flick of her hand that suggested she didn't want to be burdened with the details.

"True, it's not going to be cheap, but it could be

done in stages," Chelsea offered. "Potentially, you could fix up the interior with the plan of adding a second floor or a loft later. At least that would allow you to open for business and start bringing in some income. If there's a wedding season, you could plan the additions during the slower months or you could work around them."

Ethan did an internal double take. That sounded like a sensible plan. At least she wasn't trying to over-sell Lucy. Maybe he'd judged her too harshly. He glanced at his sister to gauge her reaction and noticed that Lucy was staring at Chelsea intently. "You look so familiar," she finally said. "Have we met before today?"

"I don't think so." Chelsea shook her head. "Maybe you've seen me in the photos at Juliette's house?"

"Maybe, but probably not," Lucy said, staring a hole through the woman. "Chelsea Allen…? Who is it that you remind me of? Even your name is familiar to me."

"I have pictures of her all over the house. That's probably where you've seen her," Juliette said. "Where were you planning on building a bride's room?"

It took Lucy a couple of beats to tear her gaze away from Chelsea.

"You do know you'll need to plan space for a bride's room," Juliette said.

"Sure. Yeah. I mean, no. I hadn't thought about it being out here. For now, we could use my house. Maybe we could build a bride's room into the plans."

"What's a bride's room?" Ethan asked. "Is that

something you can build in here, or are we talking about building another structure?"

"A bride's room is a place for the bride and her entourage to get ready before the wedding," Lucy said.

"Wouldn't she get ready at home?" The way all three women turned to look at him, he knew he'd just asked a dumb question. He didn't care. How was he supposed to know these things unless he asked?

"She might not want to put on her wedding dress before she arrives," Chelsea offered, but he must've looked confused because she continued. "Frankly, if I were getting married, I wouldn't put my gown on until just before the ceremony. It might get wrinkled or dirty. A bride's room would give her a place to dress and prepare for her wedding day. Plus, it's bad luck for the groom to see the bride before the ceremony on the day of the wedding. It would have to be out of the way so the groom doesn't see her before she walks down the aisle."

Chelsea started walking toward the north side of the barn and he followed, hearing Juliette say something to Lucy about Shay and Kyle Brighton's wedding on Saturday. The entire town had been invited, including Ethan. Even though weddings weren't his favorite thing to do on a Saturday night.

"So, you've never been married?" He had no earthly idea why he asked Chelsea that question.

"No, I haven't. Have you?"

He watched Lucy link her arm through Juliette's and steer her toward the opposite side of the barn.

They had their heads together, scheming, no doubt, as they exited the building.

"Divorced. When I got married the ceremony sure as hell wasn't in a barn."

"Barns are a newer trend in wedding venues." She stopped in a patch of sunlight that was streaming in through a shuttered window. Dust motes hung in the air, and Ethan was taken by how naturally pretty Chelsea looked in the soft afternoon light. The back-lighting made her look like an angel the way it played off her blond hair, illuminating it like a halo.

For a split second he had a crazy thought that maybe she'd been sent to save him. But as soon as the thought raced through his head he realized how pathetically asinine it was to think that and shoved it out of his brain harder than two drunks in a bar fight.

"Barns may not have been as fashionable when you tied the knot," she said. "How long ago was it?"

Even though he was the one who'd brought up marriage, he didn't want to talk about his own failed endeavor. It didn't hurt like it used to. The pain had faded once he'd gotten sober and realized that he and his ex made so much more sense as friends. It was as if sobriety had washed the letdown out of his system. In fact, now that they were divorced, he and Molly were on great terms.

"A long time ago," he finally said. "So, if wedding barns are a fad, does that mean next year something else will be all the rage and the barn will just be a barn again? Or in this case a wildly overimproved barn?"

"Not necessarily. Of course, I don't know this area, but I think a venue like this, done right, of course, will become pretty timeless. And Lucy can rent the facility for other uses besides weddings."

That was what he was afraid of. "We'll have to check into noise ordinances. Maybe that's the reason Celebration doesn't already have an outfit like this."

She shrugged. "Maybe so. It's a good idea to make sure Lucy checks into that before she spends any money."

"Or not," he said.

"Excuse me?"

"I'd rather she not do this venue thing."

Chelsea looked truly stunned. "I understand that Lucy is your sister, but she's an adult," Chelsea said. "Does she need your approval?"

"She can do whatever she wants. She doesn't need my approval."

"Not that it should matter, but Juliette believes in her. Why don't you?"

Ethan drew in a slow, measured breath. The phantom scent of hay and oats and horse hung in the air, even though it hadn't housed animals for the better part of fifteen years. "I do believe in Lucy." He stopped himself before he said too much, that he had his doubts about her ability to focus and follow through with a business like this. It was the truth, but he didn't need to share it with the world. "I have my reasons."

The words sounded a lot gruffer than he'd intended. He could tell by the way Chelsea's eyes flashed that he'd offended her.

"I'm sure you do and that's fine." She held up a hand. "It's none of my business, and I really don't want to get in the middle of it. If you'll excuse me, I'll go find Juliette and Lucy."

She turned to walk away and he should've let her go, but damned if he didn't hear himself trying to explain.

"Lucy hasn't had the best track record," he said.

Chelsea stopped and turned back toward him. Her face was neutral, but there was something in her eyes that encouraged him to keep talking.

"She's spent the past few years since our parents died searching for something that she hasn't found yet."

Chelsea's face softened. "I'm sorry for your loss."

"They've been gone for a few years now, but thank you."

The cicadas chose that moment to end the whining vibrato of their symphony. Quiet hung between Ethan and Chelsea like a sheer curtain.

"I don't want Lucy to get in over her head again," he said.

"She can't figure that out by herself?"

"She hasn't yet."

"So this isn't her first business venture, I take it?"

He shook his head.

"And let me guess, you're the big brother who steps in and always saves the day?"

"I wouldn't put it that way, but around here that's what big brothers do."

"Of course they do." The corners of her mouth turned up. He wondered how someone could look so sad when they were smiling. "I think it's universal. I have two brothers at home who always tried to fight my battles for my sister and me, too. But you know what? Sometimes a girl just has to take a chance. We don't always need to be saved. And the world doesn't end if we make a mistake now and then."

"Are you saying you've made mistakes along the way?" he asked.

"Of course I have. I'm human, Ethan."

Hearing her say his name triggered something inside him, a kind of strange tightening in his stomach. He ignored it.

"I would've taken you for someone who knows exactly what she wants and where she's going."

She shook her head. "Obviously, we don't know each other. I don't know you or your sister, but…" She hesitated a moment. "May I give you a piece of advice that will go a long way toward strengthening the brother-sister bond?"

He nodded.

"I know how it feels to come from a family that doesn't take you seriously," said Chelsea. "Lucy seems like a sweet, smart woman. Give her some credit. Don't do that to her."

"Do what to who?" Lucy asked. She and Juliette had returned.

"We were talking about planning and zoning and permits," Ethan said. "All the fun stuff."

Lucy frowned.

"We were wondering why there isn't already a venue like this in Celebration," Chelsea offered. "We were curious if maybe planning and zoning regulations were prohibitive."

"I've often wondered the same thing," Juliette said. "Why isn't there a venue here? The Regency Cypress Plantation and Botanical Gardens is just about the only game in town, unless you want to venture all the way over to Dallas. The Cypress is a good twenty miles away. Even if you're willing to drive that far, the place is booked out for nearly two and a half years. Good luck getting in in a reasonable time. Shay and Kyle booked their wedding about three years ago. Who wants to wait three years to get married?"

Juliette looked at Ethan. He shrugged.

"I have no idea," he said. "That's not my area of expertise."

"Of course, sometimes you get lucky and there's a cancellation," she continued. "Remember how fast Anna and Jake Lennox had to plan their wedding when that spot opened up all of a sudden?"

Ethan shook his head. He had no clue.

Juliette clucked. "Stop acting like you don't know what I'm talking about. You went to their wedding."

"Yeah. But how would I know about their time frame? I couldn't even tell you how long it took Molly to plan our wedding."

"Maybe that's why you're not married anymore," Lucy said.

"Ouch," he said. "Harsh, sis."

Lucy waved him off and turned to Chelsea, who was a much more accommodating sounding board than he was.

"The way I see it," Lucy said, "we will be providing a community service by opening this venue."

Juliette made noises that indicated she agreed. She turned to Chelsea.

"The Gardens are booked solid because they're the only game in town. It used to be a working sugar plantation back in the early nineteenth century. Since then, it's been refashioned into a much sought-after venue for parties and special occasions. Its history is what gives it the charm.

"When our friends Jake and Anna grabbed that unexpected cancellation, they had to put their wedding on the fast track and plan everything in three weeks. It was madness, but it was a beautiful wedding. If we do this place right, I believe we can give the Regency Cypress a run for their money."

She paused. "What do you want to call this place, Lucy?"

"I don't know. I'm still thinking about it."

"Keep thinking," Juliette said. "Because I believe our barn has so much charm that we will have a waiting list of people wanting to reserve dates, too. And, before I forget, since we will all be at Shay and Kyle's wedding on Saturday, you can see what kinds of services I provide and get an idea for some of the things we will need to think about for the renovation."

So they'd all be there? "Does that mean you're coming, too?" Ethan asked Chelsea.

She shook her head. "I wasn't invited. I don't know Shay and Kyle and I wouldn't want to crash the party."

"Nonsense," Juliette said. "I'm not going to leave you sitting at home by yourself. You can come along and help me. I can always use an extra set of hands."

"Sure, as long as I won't be in the way," Chelsea said. "I'd love to help."

First the impromptu consultation; now Jules was recruiting Chelsea to work as a wedding planning assistant. Ethan considered cracking a joke about Juliette paying her at least minimum wage, but that gave way to a warm satisfaction that she would be there. Suddenly, he wasn't dreading this wedding as much as he had been.

## Chapter Five

Chelsea had been reluctant to venture too far out into public, but it dawned on her that now that Ethan and Lucy knew she was *visiting*, it would look weird if she spent the entire time holed up inside the house. Actually, it would look downright suspicious. Besides, she was happy she could help Jules.

On Saturday morning Chelsea went with Juliette to the Regency Cypress Plantation to help her set up for the wedding reception. Apparently, the bride had someone helping her at the church. This gave Juliette and Chelsea the entire day at the reception venue. Chelsea helped with everything from stringing tiny white twinkle lights and swagging yards of tulle across the ceiling and assisting the pastry chef with the wedding cake table, to rolling up her sleeves and helping Juliette create the head table for the bridal party. She moved heavy round tables and chairs into the perfect arrangement for the guests, and after that she laid the tables with linens and place settings and the sweetest floral centerpieces made of pink peonies and white hydrangeas and sprigs of green. Wait…was that mistletoe? It sure looked like it.

"Jules, is that mistletoe in the centerpieces?"

"It is. And I'm glad you mentioned it." Juliette picked up a large box that had been pushed back into a corner. "We need to hang these mistletoe bunches in places where people can stand under them and kiss."

"But it's not Christmastime," Chelsea said. "Why are you putting up mistletoe?"

Juliette smiled. "My mission is to make dreams come true. I give the bride and groom whatever they want. Mistletoe is kind of their thing because they met at a wedding that had a mistletoe theme and they decided they wanted it at their wedding, too. Even if it is May, their wish is my command."

It was cute for a couple to have their own special tradition like that. How nice it would be to share a romantic fancy like that with your soul mate, Chelsea mused as she hung the round bunches of greenery that were interspersed with baby's breath and tied with a pink ribbon to match the flowers in the centerpieces.

By the time they'd finished setting up, Chelsea had decided that working like this was the perfect cover. Who would think to look for a humiliated British heiress behind the scenes of a Texas wedding? Besides, Americans weren't that tuned in to the UK tabloids, and even if they were, the majority wouldn't give two thoughts about her sex tape, what with the Kardashians and other reality TV stars misbehaving on a daily basis. In fact, her misadventure might even seem a bit tame comparatively. Or at least a bit anticlimactic since she hadn't tried to capitalize on the scandal. She just wanted it to go away.

It seemed that everywhere in the world, famous people or wannabe celebs had adopted the stance that bad publicity was better than being overlooked. That wasn't Chelsea's philosophy, of course, and she couldn't quite wrap her mind around the trend of relishing public shame. She simply wanted to disappear until everything had blown over and John Q. Public had forgotten her. But keeping busy like this was one step better than disappearing because while she was working, she had actually forgotten about the problem that had brought her here in the first place.

"Okay, I think we're good to go," Juliette said, standing back and surveying the room.

The place really did look fit for a princess bride with the tulle, twinkle lights and flowers, and all that mistletoe just begging people to kiss.

"This was fun. If you need a hand on other jobs while I'm here, I'm happy to help."

"Thanks, love," Jules said. "I just might take you up on that. Now, let's go change out of our work clothes and into our party dresses. The fun is about to begin."

Juliette had lent Chelsea a dress and a pair of heels to change into. Since Chelsea had packed her bags on the fly before leaving London, she'd only brought along casual clothing. She certainly hadn't foreseen attending posh events while she was away. Especially not a wedding.

However, Juliette was right about needing to freshen up and change into appropriate attire after hefting tables and hauling ladders. Chelsea was already exhausted, and the real work—when the bridal party and guests arrived for the reception—hadn't even begun. The grunt work was only the preamble. Apparently, a wedding planner's job wasn't done until the bride and groom left for their happily-ever-after and the last guest cleared the building. Chelsea had always appreciated that Juliette was a hard worker, but until now she had no idea of the amount of exhausting work required to pull off Jules's job. From the outside looking in, her friend made it seem effortless.

They changed clothes in stalls in the ladies' loo and then touched up their makeup at the communal mirror.

"You really do earn your pay, Jules," Chelsea said. "I'm impressed."

"I love my career. It simply doesn't feel like work to me."

"Well, you're darn good at it."

"Thank you. When I see my brides and grooms looking so happy, it's worth every bit of effort."

"And, of course, they pay you handsomely."

"Yes, there is that." Juliette blotted her lips, smoothing her bright pink lipstick, which looked so smart with her olive complexion. "But that's the frosting on the cake. The real compensation is loving what I do."

"You're lucky to have found your calling," Chelsea said. "I'm beginning to think that finding the perfect career might rival finding the perfect man."

The thought had her mind skittering back to Ethan Campbell and talk of his marriage to the woman named Molly. Had Ethan been Molly's perfect man? If she married him, she must've thought so in the beginning. He seemed like a decent guy, even if he was a little overly protective. Why had Molly let him get away?

"Nothing is perfect," Jules said. "Well, except for the weddings I plan. Those have to be perfect. But you'll find yourself soon enough. It was a shame what happened with Hargraves Designs."

Chelsea died a little inside. Just when she'd gotten her mind off the damn tabloid story, there it was, jumping out at her like an ugly jack-in-the-box.

Initially, Hargraves had thought her name would lend cutting edge panache to the traditional studio. She was supposed to help them connect with the younger, hipper, moneyed generation. But her stock went down the tube once the video scandal had broken. They couldn't distance themselves fast enough. In the span of hours, she'd gone from being an asset to a crushing liability. They'd gotten rid of her faster than the queen's guard would dispose of a bat caught in the royal coiffeur.

Still, she was truly thrilled for Juliette. In fact, seeing her best friend's happiness, knowing that finding one's place in the world wasn't a myth, renewed her hope.

Maybe this sojourn to Celebration would help her sort things out. At least she'd have a chance to get her head on straight. It would be nice to have some quiet time, time to hear herself think. Maybe alternating the quiet with busy days like today would help her figure out her next step.

She finished touching up her eyeliner, ran a brush through her long, blond hair and pinched her cheeks to heighten the color. With that, she decided to call it good.

"What's next?" Chelsea asked Juliette, who was gathering up her makeup and stashing it in her tote bag.

"Would you mind putting our things in the car while I do one more walk-through before the bride and groom arrive? I want to make sure I didn't miss anything?" Juliette glanced at her watch. "Guests should already be gathering in the lobby for drinks and hors d'oeuvres. The new Mr. and Mrs. should be here in the next ten minutes or so."

"I'd be happy to," Chelsea said as she hoisted her own bag up onto her shoulder and took Juliette's from her outstretched hand.

A small crowd of wedding guests had already gathered in the lobby when Chelsea left the ballroom on her way toward the parking lot. Instantly, she picked out Ethan in the crowd. He was wearing a white dress shirt with a blue tie and was holding his suit jacket. Even from this distance she could see that the tie brought out the azure of his eyes. He was a good-looking man. No wonder her gaze had automatically landed on him.

Lucy was with him, standing by the bar. She was talking to a guy with dark, wavy hair. While Lucy seemed oblivious, hanging on to the guy's every word, Ethan saw Chelsea watching them. He smiled and began walking toward her.

"Let me help you with that," he said, opening the door with his right arm and taking the two totes and garment bags with his left. They didn't weigh a ton, but they had been cumbersome enough that they would've made it challenging to juggle her load and open the doors herself. Ethan scooped them away as if they were nothing.

"Thanks," she said. Her mind skittered back to the mistletoe in the ballroom and she wondered if Ethan would kiss anyone tonight. "I was taking those to the car. I can handle them if you need to get back inside. I'm the one who is working today. You're a guest."

"I wouldn't have offered to help if I thought I might miss out on something in there," he said.

Somehow she didn't believe that. In the short amount of time she'd know Ethan, she'd learned that even though he was gruff, he always seemed willing to lend a hand.

"Well, in that case, I'll lead the way," she said. "The car is just right over there. And thanks, Ethan."

Juliette's SUV chirped when Chelsea clicked the key fob.

"You're welcome," he said as she opened the hatch

and stepped back for him to deposit the bags. "You look real pretty today. Red is a good color on you. Looks nice."

She didn't know why, but she suddenly felt shy.

She finally mustered, "Thank you. You clean up pretty well yourself." It was true. The tie and pressed white shirt was a different look for him, but he wore it well.

He smiled at her again as he slammed the hatch, and the two of them walked side by side back to the building. She caught him slanting a glance at her and she racked her brain for something to say. Why was she so bad at this? She'd always been good at making small talk. Why did he make her nervous? She wasn't a schoolgirl.

"Has Lucy given any more thought to the suggestions I made last week for the barn design?"

"I don't know. She hasn't said anything. You might want to ask her tonight. But right now she's talking to Zane Phillips. I'm sure the barn is the furthest thing from her mind."

"Zane is the guy she's with inside?"

Ethan nodded.

"Are she and Zane dating?"

His laugh was sardonic as he opened the door. "No."

His answer was so resolute she was almost sorry she asked. *Almost.*

"Don't you like the guy?"

"Of course I do. He's like a brother to me—to both of us. Come over here and I'll introduce you to him."

Scanning the crowd, she hesitated. "Maybe later? I need to get back inside and see if Juliette needs my help with anything else."

"Save me a dance?"

Something in the way he was looking at her made her nerves bunch and swarm in her stomach. The feeling took her breath away, but she managed to say, "Sounds like a plan."

Chelsea felt his gaze on her as she made her way back to the ballroom and stepped into the sanctuary of the empty hall, shutting the door behind her.

"How does the crowd look?" Juliette asked as Chelsea handed her the keys. "Are guests starting to arrive?"

"Yes, there are a lot of people out there. Tell me about Zane Phillips."

"Zane Phillips?" Juliette did a double take. "Did you meet him?"

"No, not exactly. But based on what Ethan just said, I think Lucy might have a thing for him and I'm not entirely sure Ethan is okay with that. Is he really that controlling?"

"Who, Zane?" Juliette asked as she adjusted the flowers in one of the centerpieces.

"No, Ethan."

Juliette snorted. "No, Ethan is not controlling. Not when it comes to Lucy's thing for Zane. Ethan happens to have a lot of sense when it comes to that matter. Zane loves the ladies. I'm sure you will be no exception, but he is dating someone right now—supposedly. Listen, everyone in town knows that

Lucy has had a crush on Zane for as far back as—well, for as far back as I can remember, anyway. Zane loves to flirt. Ethan's just being the protective big brother."

"How can you believe that's not controlling? He doesn't want her to date Zane. He doesn't want her to open the barn venue. Even you want her to open the barn. Help me understand."

"Ethan is a good guy, Chels. He's just a little cautious. He's endured some hard knocks with his divorce and losing his parents, but he'll come around about the barn. I mean, it just makes sense. Look at this place." She made a sweeping gesture with her hands. "It's a gold mine. Lucy has a real opportunity by giving it some competition. Even so, Ethan just wants to make sure his little sister doesn't get hurt. He holds his family tight. You can't blame a guy for that."

Chelsea didn't mean to judge. Family was everything to her, too, despite how her parents had reacted to the Hadden debacle. She and Ethan had that in common. Except in her case, she was the little sister with the overly protective siblings; she was the one who didn't measure up.

Juliette's phone dinged with a text. "The bride and groom are here. We can open the doors to the ballroom. Shay and Kyle and the bridal party will make their grand entrance in about ten minutes. If you will help me get everyone in here, then you can go enjoy yourself."

"Enjoy myself? I'm not a guest. I'm the hired help. Remember?"

"You're a volunteer," Juliette said as they moved toward the doors. "It's understood that you will be paid for your efforts in wedding cake and dances with handsome cowboys."

"Well, if you put it that way, how can I refuse? Except, I don't know the bride and groom. Won't I be one step up from a wedding crasher? I could take a cab home."

"If you can get a cab to come all the way out here, you're certainly free to go, but I wouldn't count on it. Dorothy, you're not in London anymore. We're a community here and since you're my friend, you're automatically one of us. So join the party and enjoy yourself."

Chelsea must've still looked dubious because Juliette said, "Don't worry. I'll introduce you to Shay and Kyle after they get inside and get settled."

"Okay."

Really, what choice did she have? She did suppose wedding cake and handsome cowboys sounded like the ingredients that dreams were made of, especially if it meant dancing with Ethan Campbell. And possibly two-stepping underneath a ball of that mistletoe.

That could be fun. Her stomach did that strange bunch-and-dip thing it had been doing since she first saw him.

Yeah, *uh*, no. There would be no kissing anyone tonight, no matter how tempting the mistletoe or the cowboy.

Chelsea stuck close to Juliette, helping her direct

guests who had picked up their table numbers in the lobby as they waited to enter the ballroom.

Once again, she picked Ethan out of the sea of people and noted where he was sitting—table eight. Somehow he had made it past her, either getting direction from Jules or finding his own way. It wasn't that difficult. It wasn't as if he needed a map or a guide. In addition to Lucy and Zane, two more couples were seated at the table. She wondered if someone else would be joining them to fill that open seat. Zane's girlfriend, perhaps? Ethan wouldn't have asked her to save him a dance if he was with a date. But maybe Shay would try to play matchmaker and seat a single woman at the table?

Chelsea wished she would've thought to sneak a peek at the seating chart earlier. She'd had it right in her hands when she'd set up the seating assignment table in the lobby. Of course, she could go out and ask the table attendant, Susan, for the list. However, there was no time for that because Juliette was motioning her over to meet the bride and groom.

The next half hour flew by in a series of dances—bride and groom, mother and son, father and daughter—champagne toasts and the herding of more than two hundred and fifty people through the buffet line. It was exhausting, but finally Juliette shooed Chelsea away.

"You have been such a help, but your work here is done. Now, go get something to eat."

Chelsea's stomach growled at the suggestion. She'd been so busy working she hadn't realized until now that she was ravenous. "Would you like me to make you a plate, too?"

"No, but thanks. I need to coordinate the cake cutting time with the caterer. I'll grab something later. But you go. Relax. Enjoy yourself."

With that, Juliette was off on another mission, leaving Chelsea on her own.

It appeared that all of the guests had made it through the buffet line. Chelsea went through, fixing herself a small plate with prime rib, potatoes and salad. She glanced around the room. The empty place at Ethan's table was still unoccupied. She hesitated a moment, trying to decide if she should invite herself to join him—he had asked her to find him after she was finished working and suggested they dance. But with wayward thoughts of mistletoe and cowboy kisses still lingering, maybe it would be a better idea to disappear into a quiet corner in the lobby away from everyone. In the lobby she could sit down and take off the pinching heels. The shoes were gorgeous, but Juliette's feet were half a size smaller than hers and the loaners were killing her. Not to mention, she really did feel like a fish out of water in this big ballroom full of strangers who were well acquainted with each other.

So, this was what a party looked like when you didn't belong, she thought. Except for Jules, Lucy and Ethan, the rest of the people in the room didn't know her. Of course, she would've experienced the same sensation if she had crashed a wedding in London. But Chelsea was so used to being surrounded by friends that being on the outside looking in was a strange, lonely feeling. She reminded herself that solitude was exactly what she wanted. She hadn't come to Celebration to mix and mingle and make new friends. If she knew what was best for her she would retreat into the lobby, disappear into that enticing corner and mind her aching feet.

As she turned toward the door, she noticed that Ethan looked as alone as she felt. Lucy was talking to Zane; the other couples at the table seemed to be wrapped up in their own animated conversations. And there was Ethan, eating his dinner solo in the middle of these people who were his community, his friends.

And then he caught her staring. As their gazes crashed into each other, Chelsea's stomach rose and then dropped like a falling elevator. When he waved her over, it was too late to pretend like she hadn't seen him. Really, if she was honest with herself, she didn't want to pretend. So she took her aching feet and her racing heart over to table eight.

As Chelsea approached the table, Ethan stood and pulled out the empty chair next to him.

She really did look gorgeous in that red dress. He hadn't been able to take his eyes off her since he'd entered the ballroom.

"Please join us," he said when she got closer.

His invitation drew the others out of their private conversations. They looked over to see who he was talking to. When they saw Chelsea, the guys at the table fell all over themselves standing up. It was almost like something from an old-time cartoon.

"Thank you," she said. "I hope I'm not intruding."

"Of course not," Ethan said. "Everyone, this is Chelsea Allen. She's a friend of Juliette Lowell. She was helping her out setting up for the wedding tonight."

He went around the table making introductions.

Lucy beamed at Chelsea as she put a proprietary hand on Zane's arm. For the first time, Ethan didn't mind his sister's attempt to cozy up to Zane and claim her territory. Zane was a good enough friend to know better than to mess with his sister. Zane had known Lucy long enough to know she'd always had a thing for him, but with his reputation of playing fast and loose with hearts, Ethan had faith Zane wouldn't cross that line because he'd never break Lucy's heart.

Chelsea, on the other hand, was fair game. Since Ethan had *no game* and Zane was nothing *but* game and his girlfriend wasn't here tonight, Lucy's innocent attention might level the playing field. At least it might distract Zane enough to give Ethan a head start.

*Huh.* A head start for what? Maybe he was no better than Zane in that he wasn't looking for anything more serious than some good company tonight. Did it stand to reason that since Chelsea was Juliette's friend, maybe she should be off-limits, too?

"Chelsea, I'm so glad you're here," Lucy said. "I saw you earlier, but you were busy and I didn't want to interrupt. I have so much to talk to you about. Zane, Chelsea is the fabulous interior designer I was telling you about. The one who has been giving me such great advice about converting the barn."

Ethan didn't like the greedy way Zane was devouring Chelsea with his eyes.

"An ace interior designer and a wedding planner?" Zane asked, all swagger and confidence. "Sounds like you're multitalented."

"Actually, I'm not a wedding planner at all," she said as she unfurled her napkin and placed it in her lap. "I was simply an extra pair of hands helping out tonight. And I only offered some suggestions about the barn. It was nothing groundbreaking, but I was happy to help."

"According to Lucy you helped crystallize her vision. I think she wants to hire you."

"Oh, well, no." Chelsea's cheeks colored. "I'm only visiting for a while. I couldn't commit to seeing a job through to the end. But Lucy has a brilliant mind. I'm sure she will take the suggestions I've offered and make them completely her own."

"Where are you from?" Zane asked.

"England. Jules and I went to university together."

"If you're from England, why don't you have an accent?" Lucy asked.

"I was wondering the same thing," Ethan said. "Ninety-seven percent of the time you sound American, but sometimes the way you turn words and some of the words you use sound vaguely British."

Chelsea's nose wrinkled, drawing his attention to the spray of freckles that he was becoming quite fond of. She was the perfect blend of girl-next-door sweet and sexy self-confidence.

"Like what?"

"Like saying we went to *university* together," Lucy said. "Here, we go to *college*."

"Well, in the UK, we go to university." She smiled and gave a cute quick lift of her right shoulder, one of her mannerisms that was becoming familiar. "I guess I speak the way I do because I have a lot of American friends."

"Look at her," Lucy said to no one in particular as she nodded toward Chelsea. "Who does she look like? She looks like someone and it's been driving me crazy. Who is it?"

Lucy glanced at Ethan. He shook his head. Granted, Chelsea was a beautiful woman, but she didn't remind him of anyone. She had a look that seemed unique to her alone and it, along with her mannerism and Britishisms, was only one of the things he found so alluring about her.

Lucy sighed. "It will come to me—" The music changed into a lively country tune. "Oh! I love this song. Come dance with me, Zane."

After Lucy dragged Zane onto the dance floor, goading him into some sort of group line dance, the other two couples drifted back into their worlds, leaving him and Chelsea alone amidst the wedding's jubilant chaos.

The music was loud and Chelsea was still eating her dinner; the combination made it difficult to carry on a conversation. Finally, when she set down her silverware and pushed away her plate, Ethan was at a loss for conversation starters. He'd never been one for shooting the breeze and he didn't have the patience for small talk. But sitting there imitating an uncommunicative log didn't feel right, either. So he asked her the first thing that came to mind.

"Did you hear they caught the burglar?"

"Really? The one you mistook me for?" She cocked a brow and smiled at him.

"I suppose I deserve that, but in my defense, I was only looking out for Jules. It's not every night that I catch someone breaking and entering in through the bathroom window."

"That's the only reason I'm not holding it against you."

She was surprisingly easy to talk to, blending just enough sass and good humor that he discovered she didn't take herself too seriously. Something shifted in that moment and they fell into an easy rhythm. The song ended too soon and Lucy came back without Zane. She settled herself at the table and inserted herself into their conversation.

"So, I've been thinking about getting a tattoo," Lucy said, leaning in.

*What the*— "Why do you want a tattoo?" *And more important, why do you feel the need to discuss it right now?*

"Why not, Ethan?" Lucy rolled her eyes. "Why should I expect you to understand? You've never done anything spontaneous in your entire life."

He could be spontaneous. The only reason he

wasn't was because someone had to be responsible. Their brother, Jude, was making money riding bulls for a living, and Lucy had been in school and then in California and now she was back in Celebration making noise about this barn. That left Ethan to run the family's Triple C Ranch. It was hard work that required a strict routine, and routines didn't leave much room for spontaneity.

That was fine with him.

He wasn't going to defend his work ethic. Not that it would matter. Lucy was carrying on about the tattoo again.

"Yeah, I saw this one. It was a Sanskrit saying or something like that." She was studying her fingernails as she talked. "I have no idea what it said. It was on this very classy woman." Lucy looked up and leaned in even closer, as if what she was about to say was top secret. "Okay, confession time. Tabloids are my guilty pleasure. Especially the European ones. Don't judge. I have to look at those on the internet because I can't get them here. But anyway, this poor woman got caught in a majorly compromising position, if you know what I mean."

Ethan shifted impatiently. He had no idea what she meant and frankly he didn't care. He tried to catch Lucy's eye to send the nonverbal message to stop already, but Lucy wouldn't look at him. She was talking to Chelsea.

"Yeah, the story was something about her ex-boyfriend going rogue and publishing their sex tape.

Pretty humiliating, huh? But I digress. That's how I saw her tat."

Oh, hell. He loved his sister, but sometimes she had no shame. Why the hell was she talking about sex tapes and tattoos at a wedding and with someone she barely knew? Chelsea was obviously embarrassed by it because she had turned as pale as the white tablecloth and was sitting ramrod straight in her chair.

"Lucy, really?" Ethan said. "Stop." He turned to Chelsea. "I apologize on her behalf—"

"No, it's okay, Ethan." Chelsea cleared her throat. "So, Lucy, did you actually watch this tape?"

Lucy scrunched up her face as if she was truly disgusted by the suggestion—despite the fact that she was the one who brought up the subject.

"Oh! No way. I didn't want to watch it. Plus, I was afraid if I clicked on it I would get a virus on my computer or my phone. Is it possible to get a virus on your phone?"

*"Yes,"* Chelsea insisted. "Be careful about that. Phone viruses will erase all your photos and contacts and steal all your passwords."

Hmm. He'd never heard of a phone virus, and he had a sneaking suspicion Chelsea was messing with Lucy, which would serve her right.

"Don't watch things like that, okay?" Chelsea said. "No good can come of it. If this so-called boyfriend released that tape without the woman's consent— that's just wrong. Sometimes guys do that to shame women. It's just wrong."

*What kind of a jerk would do something like that?*

"I did see the pictures, though." Lucy shrugged and she pursed her lips. "That's how I saw this *particular* tattoo. I mean, it was really different. It was *classy.*"

"Lucy, just stop, okay?" Ethan said. He looked around, trying to locate Zane, hoping he would come back and distract Lucy. Right about now he would pay him to dance with his sister.

"A lot of people have Sanskrit tattoos," Chelsea said. "It's sort of a thing right now. Everybody's getting them."

"Everybody?" Lucy said. "Does that mean you have a Sanskrit tattoo?"

"Seriously, Lucy," he said. "Stop. End of this discussion. Chelsea, how about that dance you promised me?"

Lucy knew.

She *knew.*

*Bloody hell.* She'd figured it out and Chelsea was nearly paralyzed by the thought of what Lucy might do with that info.

Her heart thumped wildly and her legs felt like rubber as she followed Ethan out onto the dance floor away from Lucy. If Ethan hadn't asked her to dance, would Lucy have aired that bit of dirty laundry right there in front of everyone?

The grilling about her accent was bad enough. The fake American accent thing was only supposed to be used on rare occasion and when she was in a predicament. The Chelsea Allen persona was a

means to an end, an alter ego to throw people—
mostly drunk men—off the scent of Lady Chelsea
Ashford Alden. If she had known she would be in-
teracting with Juliette's friends—if Ethan hadn't surprised her and thrown her into survival mode—she
would've thought better of using the fake accent. Now
she was stuck, because she couldn't very well tell
them she was just kidding. Life tended to get messy
when things got real.

The only reason she hadn't excused herself from
this conversation was because she thought playing it
cool might throw Lucy off. Of course, she didn't have
a way to get back to Juliette's until the wedding was
over and it was too late to hide in the lobby corner,
but that was beside the point. If she left the reception
now, even to take a long walk around the grounds,
she'd all but confirm Lucy's theory that she was, in-
deed, the hapless woman with the *classy* tattoo.

A spiral of Sanskrit words inked permanently on
her derriere.

As if the situation couldn't get worse, the music
shifted to a slow tune as they stepped onto the dance
floor. Ethan didn't give her time to object. He simply
pulled her into his arms and they proceeded to sway
to the country ballad.

"I'm sorry about what happened back there at the
table," he said. "I hope she didn't embarrass you."

He smelled good.

His cheek rested against her temple. The nearness
of him, the feel of his solid arms around her, gave
her the momentary delusion that she was safe. If she
closed her eyes and blocked out everything but the

feel of him and the smell of his citrusy aftershave, she could believe it. Well, if not for that compulsive voice in her head reminding her she was anything but safe, because wild card Lucy could expose her at whim.

In a sense she was safer on the dance floor...in Ethan's arms.

"Your sister does tend to fixate on things, doesn't she?"

"That's what I've been trying to tell you. She can be pretty intense."

"Do you have any other brothers and sisters?" Chelsea asked, eager to change the subject.

"A brother, Jude. He's a professional bull rider, off traveling the world."

"Two cowboys in one family?" she said. "You dance very well, considering."

"Considering what?"

"Considering I thought cowboys only two-stepped."

"Don't believe all the tall tales you hear," he said.

"Are you going to shatter my romantic notions?"

"You're a romantic, are you?" he asked.

He shifted his hand to the small of her back. She could feel the warmth of him and it unleashed a shiver of something that resembled desire.

"I suppose I was once. Not anymore."

"Why not? Did another cowboy ride off with your heart?"

*No. Hadden Hastings was about as far from a cowboy as a man could be and—* "I've told you something you didn't know about me. Now it's your turn to tell me something I don't know about you."

"Like what?"

She thought for a moment. As she did, her gaze drifted to the table. Lucy wasn't sitting there anymore and Chelsea couldn't decide if that was a good thing or not.

"Have you lived anywhere other than Celebration?" she finally asked.

"I moved to Chicago right after college."

"Chicago? That's a surprise."

"Why?"

"I guess I never pegged you for a big city kind of guy. What brought you to Chicago?"

She felt him stiffen a little and pull back ever so slightly. "My wife got a job. It was an offer we couldn't refuse."

*His wife. Oh.*

Inviting the specter of his wife was a sure way to kill any possible romantic notions. Maybe that wasn't such a bad thing. So she gave in to that part of her that was overrun with morbid curiosity and could not close the door on his past.

"Her name was Molly, right? You mentioned her that day at the barn."

"Yep."

"What was her job?"

He was quiet long enough for Chelsea to wonder if she was being too nosy.

"I'm sorry," she said. "We don't have to talk about it if it makes you uncomfortable."

"No, it's okay. She and I are still good friends. I don't mind talking about her. She is a pharmaceutical sales rep and she still lives in Chicago. We were high school sweethearts and we were probably too young to realize we had no business getting married since we didn't even know who we were or what we wanted out of life, but that didn't stop us. We got hitched right out of college. We had agreed that we would stay in Celebration and take over the Triple C, my family's ranch."

"Triple C?" she asked. "Does C stand for Campbell?"

"It does. My granddad was the one who founded the ranch. He named it after my dad and his brothers. I always wanted to come back here after college and work with the horses. But Molly wanted the big city."

"I love horses. It's been so long since I've been riding."

"We'll have to go sometime."

"Thank you. I would love that."

She stared up into his blue, blue eyes as they swayed together to the slow country love song. The singer was crooning something about his eyes being the only thing he didn't want to take off his lover. In a flash she imagined Ethan undressing her. The feel of Ethan's hand on the small of her back and the thought of him making love to her sent a ripple of longing shivering through her.

She needed to get the conversation back on platonic ground. The best way to do that was to talk about his ex-wife.

"I'm sorry, I interrupted you with questions about the ranch. So you wanted to stay in Celebration, but you ended up moving to Chicago?"

"Yes. Molly's dream job came along and we moved

to Chicago. We came back to Celebration and we got a divorce." He shrugged, as if shaking off the hurt. "That's when I learned you could love someone but never really know that person. I thought we wanted the same things. But we didn't. It sort of felt like bait and switch. But in the end I knew one of us was going to be miserable if we stayed together." He shrugged again. "We were just kids when we made those plans. People change. How can you know someone who doesn't even know what she wants?"

His words hit home. She didn't know what to say. So she waited for him to continue, but he didn't. So they danced, silently swaying to the love song.

Finally, he asked, "What about you? What's your story?"

On some level, she'd known a question like that was coming. That's how intimacy worked. When two people were getting to know each other and one confided something personal… She knew it was her turn to offer something…to meet him halfway by sharing something of herself. But what was she supposed to say about herself? No, it wasn't a good idea to encourage this…this…whatever it was that made her want to put her head on his shoulder and lose herself in him.

Her trepidation was validated when she spied the wedding photographer snapping pictures of people on the dance floor. Lucy had shattered her false sense of security when she'd recognized her; there was a chance others might be familiar with the scandal, too. That's why Chelsea didn't want her picture in Shay and Kyle's wedding album.

"My story is I would love another glass of wine," she said, turning her back to the camera. "Let's go get something to drink and I will tell you anything you want to know."

*Within reason*, she added silently.

With the photographer on the loose, Chelsea wanted to stay a safe distance away. She couldn't take any more chances.

Ethan handed her a glass of red wine and he sipped something clear and bubbly.

"Is that club soda?" She gestured to his glass.

"It is."

"Are you the designated driver?"

"Actually, I don't drink. Alcohol and I don't get along."

"If this bothers you—" she held up her glass "—I can have club soda, too. Or just water."

"The only thing that'll bother me is if you don't enjoy your wine."

"Are you sure?"

He nodded.

"Fair enough," she said, feeling a little awkward about touching her wineglass to his seltzer water, but knowing it would be worse if she didn't.

It took a strong man to admit that he and alcohol didn't get along. She found his honesty refreshing. Apparently, there was more to Ethan Campbell than first met the eye, complex layers that ran much deeper than she'd realized. She realized how little she knew about him and how much more she wanted to know. But for now, this was a good start.

She turned to him and said, "I promised you my story in exchange for wine. What do you want to know?"

He was just opening his mouth to speak when one of the bridesmaids materialized. "You do know you're standing under the mistletoe, right?" She pointed toward the ceiling. Ethan and Chelsea both looked up. Sure enough, they had planted themselves right under one of the green orbs.

Those who were around them started chanting, "Kiss! Kiss! Kiss! Kiss!"

Before she even knew what was happening, Ethan placed his hand on the back of her neck, leaned in and pressed his lips to hers.

It was a tender kiss. Whisper-soft, but lingering. He tasted of lemons from his club soda and something else that was uniquely him…and quite delicious. For a moment the entire world telescoped and disappeared until it was just the two of them, his lips on hers, his warm hand, which had somehow slipped beneath her hair to rest, skin on skin, on the back of her neck.

A bright flash of light shocked her senses and dropped her with a thud back in the here and now. When Chelsea pulled away from Ethan, she blinked at the sight of Lucy standing there with her cell phone aimed at them.

"Smile, you two," Lucy said. The flash blinded them as she snapped yet another shot.

## Chapter Six

The kiss had rocked Chelsea's world, shaken her down to the core. Much more than she cared to admit. It was a kiss that she'd felt all the way to the center of her. But then she'd realized they had an audience and their kiss had been captured in a photograph. She'd murmured something about needing to catch up with Juliette and had beaten a hasty retreat. Ethan hadn't come after her, making it pretty clear that he, too, was fine putting some distance between them.

However, Lucy seemed eager to talk when she caught up with Chelsea.

"Come take a walk with me," Lucy said. "I think you need to get some air."

They'd gone outside and walked past the porte cochere to a bench next to the fountain in the center of the driveway. They were far enough away from the valets and guests who were leaving early that they wouldn't be overheard. The sound of the water and the noise of purring car engines provided an extra sound screen to give them enough privacy to talk.

Lucy spoke first.

"Lady Chelsea Ashford Alden, I presume. Should I curtsy or something? Because you're royalty, aren't you?"

"Bloody hell," Chelsea muttered under her breath in full accent. A wave of nausea rippled through her. She had forgotten how awful it felt to face people who knew about her fall from grace, people who had seen the evidence. "No, I'm not royal."

"But you have a title."

"That's because my father is the Earl of Downing. Lucy, what are you going to do with those pictures?"

Lucy shot her a smug look.

"Erase them, please," Chelsea demanded.

"No, they're great," Lucy said as she scrolled through them on her phone. "Here, look."

She held out the cell so that Chelsea could see, but stopped short of handing her the phone.

Sure enough, there she and Ethan were, locking lips. She started to breathe a sigh of relief because in the shot, Ethan's face was blocking hers. He could've been kissing any blond woman in a red dress. But it was the second shot that sent the premature sense of relief sailing right out the proverbial window. In that picture, both she and Ethan were squinting right at the camera, looking like wildlife caught in headlights.

When you put the two photos side by side, there was no mistake who Ethan Campbell had been kissing in the first picture.

"What do you plan to do with the pictures, Lucy?"

"I haven't decided yet."

"Please don't put them on social media." She hated how desperate her voice sounded.

"Why not?" Lucy asked coyly.

"For obvious reasons. You know what I'm talking about." Oh, dear God, Lucy already knew about her predicament. Was she going to have to spell it out for her? She really had hoped that she would've exercised a little compassion. Actually, Chelsea still couldn't tell what her motivation was, if she was just getting a kick out of torturing her or if she really did have plans for the photos—like extortion.

Chelsea cleared her throat, trying to dislodge the lump of frustration and panic that was nearly choking her. "I came to Celebration to get away from the press. I wanted to get out of the public eye so I could get my life back together. When the *Tattler* released that video clip, it not only turned my life upside down, but it hurt my family, too. If you publish those pictures— even on social media—I'm afraid chaos will start up all over again. Will you please take pity on me and delete them?"

"But it's such a good picture of you and my brother. I haven't seen him look this happy in ages."

"He looks startled. He doesn't look happy. Neither of us looks happy in those pictures. Look, Lucy, what do you want from me?"

Lucy was looking down at her phone again. "It's simple, really. I want your design services."

"I'm already helping you. Are you blackmailing me?"

"Why?" She looked up at Chelsea with big, innocent eyes. "Would it work if I did?"

Now it was Chelsea's turn to stare at Lucy, and she was sure she was looking at her as if she had two heads, but Chelsea really was at a profound loss for words.

Lucy must've noticed how uncomfortable Chelsea felt because she immediately said, "I'll pay you, of course. It's not like I'm trying to blackmail design services out of you."

"But you are implying if I choose not to continue with your project then you'll plaster the photos of me kissing your brother all over the internet?"

"You don't have to put it that way."

"But that seems to be the only offer on the table."

"You don't have to make it sound so criminal. I've always believed that when you do something for a friend the friend should do something for you. I'll keep the photos and your identity safe, you help me get my barn in shape to open."

"I didn't realize we were friends."

"Of course we are. And we're going to be even better friends by the time this is over. Plus, there's a special built-in bonus just for you. You'll get to spend more time with my brother. I think you two make an adorable couple."

Couple? One kiss under the mistletoe at a spring

wedding did not make them a couple. She thought about asking Lucy what Ethan would think of her little game of extortion. She also thought about simply pulling the phone out of Lucy's hands and deleting the photos herself, but instead she opted for a more sensible right of refusal.

"I'm not licensed to work as an interior designer in the US."

"You don't have to be licensed. I'm not asking you to take down walls."

"But you were talking about adding that second story. I can't help you with that."

"Someone else can handle that part, Lady Chelsea."

"Please don't call me that."

"Why not? If I had a title, I'd insist people called me Lady Lucy. Not only do you have the title, you have the vision to get my barn into shape. You described exactly what I want. I'm not asking you to stay forever. That would be up to you and my brother. Still, can't you think of this as a win-win? I get my barn designed and you get to spend more time with my Ethan."

The crazy thing was Lucy's win-win didn't sound altogether bad. She had to admit that she was excited about the kiss—*er*—the *project*. Yes, the *project*. She'd never had a chance to see a design task through from start to finish. At least it would be a way that she could keep herself busy when she wasn't helping Juliette. And, in a sense, helping Lucy pull this old barn into shape so that she could open the

wedding venue in Celebration would also be helping out Juliette, because it would give her a venue
closer to home.

"We might be able to work out a deal, but I need
something from you, Lucy."

"Anything. Just name it."

"I need for you to give me your word that not only
will you not sell or post those photos anywhere, you
also have to promise me that you will keep my secret, too. Juliette knows, but I don't want anyone else
in Celebration to know the reason I'm here. Do we
have a deal?"

"I can't promise that nobody else in Celebration
reads the British tabloids, but you have my word that
I will not sell you out. I won't tell anyone else what I
know about you and I won't sell or post the pictures."

Lucy stuck out her hand. As the cool evening breeze
ruffled the nearby hedges, Chelsea regarded Lucy's
proffered hand for a moment. She wanted to believe
her. She seemed like she was pretty up front about
everything. Maybe Chelsea was naive, but she really
wanted to believe Lucy was a decent person.

To prove as much, she shook her hand.

"Actually, as a show of good faith and in the spirit
of working together, I'd like for you to delete the
photos right now."

A mischievous look colored Lucy's eyes. "I'll do
one better. I'll send them to you and erase them on
my phone. Because I'm willing to bet that not too long
from now you're going to want a picture of your first
kiss with my brother. What's your phone number?

I mean, I'm going to need your number anyway if we're going to be working together. Giving me your number will be your good faith gesture."

As Chelsea rattled off her digits, the whole bizarre situation struck her as funny. Nothing in her life had ever been conventional. Not even her first independent design job, where a photo of a first kiss served as the contract.

The photos came through on a ping, and Chelsea checked to make sure she'd received them both. When she looked up, she saw Lucy holding up her phone and, one by one, sending the pictures to the trash can icon.

"They're gone, okay? I mean, you can check my phone if you want."

Chelsea took Lucy's phone and scrolled through all the photo albums. There were several selfies of Lucy making silly faces, a couple of shots of the barn, photos of Lucy with some girlfriends and a few from tonight of her and Zane with their heads together.

They really would make a handsome couple. But the two of Chelsea and Ethan were gone. They weren't even in the recently deleted bin.

She handed the phone back to Lucy.

"Are we good then?"

Chelsea nodded.

Lucy drummed her manicured nails on her phone case. She looked as if she wanted to say something. But Chelsea remained quiet, letting her speak first.

"I don't want you to think that I really would

blackmail you. Obviously, you don't have to do this if you don't want to."

"I don't mind helping you, Lucy. You and I are sort of kindred spirits. I know you've been searching for your place. Juliette really thinks this wedding barn might be a good thing for you."

"I love the sentiment," Lucy said. "But how exactly does that make us kindred spirits?"

"Because I understand what it's like to be searching and how it feels when no one takes you seriously."

Chelsea told Lucy about her successful siblings and how her ex's releasing the tape had cast a shadow over her entire family. That was why she'd left London. The embarrassment that had made her sick to her stomach had nearly paralyzed her when she realized the way it affected her family.

"I'm sorry, but I just have to ask," Lucy said when she was finished doing as she promised. "Why did you let the creep film you if you didn't want it splashed all over the internet? Nowadays, you just can't be too careful or too trusting."

"I didn't know he was filming me," Chelsea said. "We'd been dating a while. I never dreamed he would do something like that. I trusted him. Am I foolish to trust you?"

"No! You *can* trust me," Lucy said.

"I hope so, because if you tell anyone who I really am, word is bound to get around. If the press shows up I'll have to leave Celebration. I won't be able to finish your barn."

"I understand."

"If the press does get wind—even if it's not your fault—you understand I'll have to leave. I decided to come to Celebration and stay with Juliette because I didn't want to hide out in my flat in London. Celebration is a much smaller town than London. If anyone gets wind of this, I'll have no choice but to leave."

"I already told you, your secret is safe with me. I promise I will not say a word to anyone. But you might want to think about confiding in Ethan. He's a good guy and he could be a great source of support."

That was exactly what she was worried about and that was exactly why she wouldn't be confiding in Ethan. She could get used to kisses like that, and that was the last thing she needed right now.

"There you are." The sound of Ethan's voice breaking through the night air as if they had conjured him startled her even more than seeing the camera flash go off. Concern commandeered his features as he looked back and forth between Lucy and her. "I've been looking all over for you two. Is everything okay?"

## Chapter Seven

Ethan couldn't stop thinking about that kiss. It had been spontaneous and she'd kissed him back as if she'd liked it as much as he had. But then she'd gotten spooked when the damn camera flash went off. When he'd found her outside by the fountain with Lucy, she'd asked him to take her home because she wasn't feeling well.

The drive was mostly silent. He wasn't sure if he should apologize for kissing her. The only reason he didn't was if she truly was angry at him, would she have gotten in his truck for a half-hour ride back to Celebration?

As she stared out the passenger window, he'd pondered all these things as they drove through the inky night.

Where was she hiding that fancy tattoo? Based on

her reaction to Lucy, Ethan was sure Chelsea had one somewhere on that body.

When they'd reached Juliette's house, he'd walked her up to the door. His instincts had told him to give her space, not to kiss her, even though he ached to taste those lips again.

Instead, he joked, "Are you using the front door or the bathroom window tonight? I can give you a boost if it's the latter. I pride myself on being a gentleman like that."

"You're a funny guy, Ethan Campbell." She held up a key ring, letting it dangle between them. For a moment the way she looked at him made him think she just might lean in herself. Maybe even invite him inside. But then she closed that figurative door. "And you are most definitely a gentleman. Thank you for rescuing me. Good night."

It was fine. He could respect that. It was probably for the best. He wasn't looking for anything permanent. She was only visiting Celebration. Who knew how long she would be there?

He had no idea what was going on inside that pretty head of hers, but the kiss proved—at least to himself—he was not a stick-in-the-mud.

If he was honest with himself, tonight something had awakened inside him. He was feeling things he hadn't felt in a very long time. While he wasn't looking to fall in love, spending more time with Chelsea Allen just might be the cure for his *old man syndrome*, a condition that he was just realizing he'd been suffering. He and Molly had been divorced for five years now; he'd been sober for more than two years. Somehow in that time he had stopped living. Life— that was what he'd felt in Chelsea's kiss. She had such a zest for life—maybe some of that zest would rub off on him. Since she wouldn't be there long, maybe they could see each other. She just might be a good interim step in the right direction. Someone to prime the pump, get him back out there in the world again. But he knew he needed to take it slow.

The Triple C was a relative newcomer compared to other ranches in the area. Ethan's granddad had started the business back in the '40s. After his grand-dad had passed, Ethan's dad, Leroy, had inherited the ranch along with the responsibility to nurture and grow the ranch so that future generations of Camp-bells might continue the legacy. The only problem was that Leroy loved the bottle more than the busi-ness and his drinking began to get in the way. After a while, the only thing that kept the Triple C afloat were the good people that Leroy had working for him. Or so Ethan thought. But after the car accident, which killed Leroy and paralyzed his mother, Ethan realized the business was in worse shape than it ap-peared on the surface.

That was a period of time when his whole world seemed to be crashing down around him. The way he dealt with it was by following in his old man's foot-steps and numbing the pain. He'd nearly followed in his old man's footsteps by finishing off the job of destroying the Triple C Ranch. Thank God he'd woken up and chosen to get himself sober before he lost everything.

He hadn't always been unspontaneous. There was a time when he'd loved nothing more than to laugh and have a good time with friends over drinks. When his marriage started heading south, the drinks blotted out the pain and blurred the reality of just how unhappy he and Molly were together. That was a long time ago. He was a new man. Now the only way to stay on track was to stay on schedule. He got up at five thirty every morning, showered, dressed and brewed himself a big cup of joe. He was in his truck by six fifteen, ready to start his daily rounds of the ranch's 900 acres. The pastures and breeding barns were confined to the 300 acres he'd inherited, but he enjoyed touring the entire property for reasons both practical and spiritual.

He liked to drive around the Campbell land not only to experience the sheer beauty of it but also to remind him of how blessed he was to have inherited the operation and how close he came to losing it before he'd gotten sober. If ever he was tempted to take a drink when he was stressed or tired or lonely, all he had to do was jump in his truck and take in the visual reminder of his blessings. It was better than any twelve-step program—well, maybe not better, but it was a good kick in the ass when he needed to get back on track.

On regular days, when he toured the Triple C, he kept an eye out for things that might cause concern—

signs of predators, an anxious horse, a broken fence, a mare that might not be bonding with her foal. He reported the problems to his assistant manager, who made sure the issue was fixed.

After he finished his morning rounds, Ethan usually returned to his office, where he would spend a couple of hours answering emails, poring over results of races in which the ranch's progeny ran and reviewing the veterinarians' reports of which mares were in foal and which were heading out to the breeding shed that day.

That Monday Ethan finished his morning's work around nine o'clock. He went into the office kitchen, filled two metal to-go cups with coffee, grabbed a couple of muffins that his bookkeeper, Allison, had brought in that morning and drove over to the barn on Lucy's property.

Saturday night when he'd taken her home, Chelsea had mentioned that she was going to head over to the barn this morning to help get Lucy started.

Saturday night things between them felt tenuous— as if it might be the beginning of something good or if there was too much pressure it might all go up in smoke. If he came on too strong he might ruin everything.

So silence had reigned.

Today, however, was a new day. Even if he still felt her kiss on his lips and the mystery of her secret tattoo still haunted him, they needed to talk about the barn before this project got too far out of hand.

\* \* \*

Chelsea jumped at the sound of the barn door opening behind her.

She whirled around to see Ethan sporting two cups of something and a small brown paper bag.

"Good morning," he said. "I thought I might find you here."

"I guess so." She gestured to the goods he was holding. "Either me or someone else. What do you have there?"

He held out one of the cups as he approached. "I come bearing gifts."

"Aw, you shouldn't have. But I'm glad you did. Thank you. I could use a break right now. I've been here since about seven o'clock."

"Alone?"

Chelsea nodded.

"Where is my sister? Why isn't she helping you?"

"She'll be in a little later."

Lucy had texted her last night with some good news. After she'd gone back into the reception, she'd run into Connor Bryce, who, according to Lucy, was an old family friend. She mentioned something about his being a wheelchair-bound veteran who had recently met and proposed to the love of his life. Saturday night at Shay and Kyle Brighton's wedding, Lucy had talked Connor and his fiancée into considering her barn for their ceremony and reception. She was having breakfast with them at eight o'clock this morning. Since everything was so new and up in the air, she had specifically asked Chelsea not to mention the meeting to anyone. Not Juliette and especially not Ethan. In fact, the only reason she told Chelsea was because they were supposed to meet at the barn this morning. Chelsea had cheered her on and assured her that she was fine getting started without her. After all, if you didn't have business, there was no use having a venue.

Of course, she didn't know Lucy very well, but aside from the pseudo-blackmail stunt, this go-getter attitude made her seem a lot more responsible and on the ball than people gave her credit for. Of course, the proof would be in the results, but they hadn't even finalized the concept, and Lucy was already out securing clients. Time would tell.

"This is exactly what I was afraid of. There's work to be done and Lucy is nowhere to be found."

Chelsea waved him off.

"Don't be so hard on her. Because really, it's fine. In fact, I was enjoying the peace and quiet."

"Until I barged in."

One side of his mouth quirked up. She was beginning to realize Ethan Campbell had a dry sense of humor that she didn't always get at first. But at least he *had* a sense of humor.

"I don't know yet," she said. "It depends on what's in the bag."

She pointed to the brown paper bag he was still clutching in his left hand.

Smiling, he said, "You don't miss anything, do you?"

She lifted her chin and shook her head.

He handed her the bag. "Actually, these muffins are something that shouldn't be missed. The Triple C's bookkeeper, Allison, makes them from scratch. She calls them chocolate pecan pie muffins."

Chelsea peered into the bag. "Oh, Lord, that sounds like an addiction waiting to happen." She claimed one and handed the bag back to Ethan.

"I think we need to sit down and give these our full reverence," she said. "Do you have time?"

"If I didn't, I'd make time."

Chelsea blinked; her heart stuttered but she refused to read anything into his words. Or into the fact that he had brought her coffee and a sinfully delicious breakfast treat.

"Let's sit over here." She gestured to an old army trunk that was one of the few things still inside the barn other than a ladder, some sawhorses and an old shovel.

The trunk wasn't very big, so their knees knocked when they sat down. Neither of them seemed in any hurry to give the other more personal space.

They sat there in companionable silence, enjoying the coffee. And he was right, the chocolate pecan pie muffin was to die for.

"This is so good. Why haven't you married her, Ethan? Anyone who makes muffins like this would surely make the perfect wife."

"Someone beat me to the punch. Otherwise, I just might. Though people might gossip about the age difference. She could be my grandmother."

"I suppose you wouldn't want to cause a stir."

"Speaking of potentially causing a stir, I'm concerned that Lucy isn't here helping you. This is sort of par for the course for her."

Chelsea turned to face him. Now the top of her calf was pressed against his upper thigh. Real or imagined, she could feel the heat of his body seeping into hers. "Will you do me a favor?"

"Anything."

"Have some faith in your sister. I think you will be pleasantly surprised. I hope you will. But you have to give her a chance to prove herself."

He regarded her for a moment and she could see the wheels turning in his head. She figured he was probably doing his best to choose his words wisely.

"You are my sister's biggest advocate. Do you always root for the underdog?"

"I suppose I could turn the tables and ask if you always expect the worst of people. But somehow I think you're just particularly hard on your sister. Ethan, Lucy will live down to your expectations and she would probably live up to them if you gave her some credit."

"I'm trying to be realistic."

"I understand. I was always the underdog of my family. I know how it feels when everyone expects the worst of you."

Ethan scowled as if he found that hard to believe.

"The other day you said your brothers don't take you seriously, but that's not the same thing as expecting the worst of you."

Chelsea shrugged. She felt as if she was dancing

along a dangerously fine line between explaining her reasoning and telling him too much.

"All I'm saying is I know how it feels to have a family who doesn't respect what you do."

"How can they not respect what you do? You have talent. I can see it, even in the few suggestions you've given Lucy."

He raised his brow and stared off into the distance somewhere as if he was processing everything. For a moment she worried that maybe she had overstepped. She half expected him to ask who she thought she was to come in and stir things up when her own life was such a mess. Then again, Ethan didn't know that about her and she needed to take care to keep it that way.

"If I am hard on her, it's only because I care. I don't want to see her get hurt. I don't like to see the people I care about get hurt."

He reached out and tucked a strand of hair that had escaped her ponytail behind her left ear. For a moment she thought he was going to lean in and kiss her again. Like he had Saturday night. Today it was just the two of them alone in the barn. No mistletoe. No people goading them. No cameras to capture the moment. Just the two of them doing this unsure pas de deux. She didn't know why they were both so nervous.

It was just a kiss. And what a kiss it had been.

When she had been alone with her thoughts yesterday and the memory of his lips was still fresh, all she could think about was how they'd lost themselves for a moment, how she'd lost herself and momentarily forgotten how Hadden had betrayed her.

Now they were talking around it—about everything but the kiss. It seemed like they were pretending it had never happened.

She reminded herself that she was in no position to get involved with anyone. Even so, if he leaned in right now and kissed her again, she'd let him.

Except Lucy chose that moment to push through the door.

"Chelsea? Oh, Ethan! Good! You're both here." Her exuberance shattered the spell between Chelsea and Ethan. They managed to find the personal space that just moments before had seemed nonexistent. "I have great news."

Chelsea could tell by the way Lucy was nearly brimming over that the meeting with the potential first client must have gone well.

"Let's hear it," Chelsea said. "Don't keep us waiting."

Lucy shot Chelsea a knowing look, but proceeded to deliver the news as if it was a surprise for both of them.

"Are you ready for this?" She didn't wait for them to answer. "Put away all your doubts, dear brother. I have secured my very first client for the *Campbell Wedding Barn*. Do you like the name? That's new, too. I had to name the place since this is really going to happen."

"Details, please," said Chelsea. She glanced at

Ethan, who was looking dubious, impervious to Lucy's effervescence.

"Ethan, Connor Bryce and his fiancée have agreed to be my very first clients and have their wedding and reception at the Campbell Wedding Barn. They are going to come out for a tour next week."

Ethan flinched. "Are you kidding? I mean congratulations on scoring your first gig, but aren't you afraid you might scare them off if you show them the place looking like this?"

Lucy shook her head. "I warned them that they would have to come with an open mind, that the place would be undergoing renovation soon. They promised to bring their imagination, and I promised to give them a discount."

Chelsea was holding her breath, waiting for Ethan's response. Lucy must've been doing the same because the place was unnervingly quiet.

"Did you discuss dates?" Ethan asked.

"We did. They want to get married next month."

"That's impossible," Ethan said. "How in the world are we going to get the barn in shape in a month? The plans that you have been discussing could take six months to complete. For that matter, you don't even have plans drawn up or permits drawn. I just don't see how we can do it."

Even though he was being pessimistic, the fact that he kept saying *we* was a good sign.

"I believe we can do this," Chelsea said. "I'm not licensed in Texas, but I can draft the plans and we can get an architect to pretty them up and sign off on them. It should be enough for permitting—at least according to what I read when I looked it up."

Again, Lucy and Chelsea were holding their breaths, waiting for Ethan's reaction. Of course, Lucy didn't need his approval, but Chelsea already understood that family unity was important to these two.

Ethan's face softened. He shrugged. "How soon do you think you can have the drafting done?"

"If Lucy and I can finalize the design, I can draft up the plans using a program I have on my laptop. I can finish it in a day or so."

"Of course, we will pay you," Ethan said.

"Since I'm not licensed, I don't know if that's even legal. Please consider my design services my business-warming gift to you."

Looking a little skeptical yet resigned, Ethan said, "Looks like we have our work cut out for us. Let me know when the plans are ready and I will help get them to the right people down at City Hall so we can expedite the permitting process. Right now I have to get back to work.

"I'll talk to you later," Ethan said to Chelsea. Then he turned to Lucy, "I'm proud of you, sis."

After Ethan had shut the doors, Lucy squealed, grabbed Chelsea's hands and began jumping up and down.

"This is really real." She stopped jumping. "Or if it's a dream, don't wake me up because I don't want to know."

Chelsea smiled at her. "It's as real as you want to

make it, Lucy. The power is in your hands and you're off to a great start."

Lucy looked around the place dreamily. "When I walked in, you and Ethan looked like you were getting cozy." She smiled. "I told you this would be a win-win."

"I have no idea what you're talking about." Chelsea tried not to smile, but she was having a hard time. "Even so. We'll make this happen."

"Are you talking about the barn," Lucy asked, "or your romance with Ethan?"

## Chapter Eight

Chelsea was a woman of her word, Ethan thought as he held open the door of City Hall and they stepped out into the sunny spring morning. She and Lucy had finalized a simple design that required minimal construction and could be completed within a few weeks if they all pulled together and worked hard.

Chelsea had drafted the plans in record time. Lucy had prevailed upon an architect friend to look over the drawings. After the guy had signed off and rubber-stamped it, Ethan and Chelsea handed the blueprints off to the permitting department. Lucy had offered to come, but Ethan had given her a pass for selfish reasons. He wanted to be alone with Chelsea.

The clerk had promised it wouldn't take very long to get an answer—a day or two at the most. First of the week at the very latest, since the planning and zoning committee was meeting on Thursday.

They'd done all the paperwork. Now they waited.

"That seemed easy," Chelsea said. Her perfume, something light and floral, teased his senses as she walked next to him down the sidewalk in downtown Celebration.

"I'd hold off on making that comment until after we get the permits," Ethan said.

Chelsea wrinkled her nose, and the way she looked made his heart compress and then beat a little faster. "Do you foresee there being a problem?"

"No. I hope not. You just never know with bureaucracies. Especially since this is a two-part process. Not only are we asking them to approve the building plan that you so graciously helped Lucy bring to life, but we're also asking for a zoning variance for the property. As it stands the barn is zoned for private use, but the more I looked into it I don't think we should have a problem because the Triple C is zoned commercial. Even though we generally don't have parties in the breeding barns—or at least not the kind of parties we're talking about—I'm hoping the area of the ranch that is zoned commercial will set a precedent."

"Let's hope for the best. You seem pretty connected with all those bureaucrats. If it's based on popularity, you shouldn't have a problem."

Ethan didn't know why but he found it satisfying that she saw him in a favorable light. Maybe it was because they'd gotten off to such a rocky start when they first met. She was too polite to say it, but it was obvious she thought he was a hard-ass. Of course, he thought she was breaking into Juliette's house, but looking back on the situation, even he thought he needed to lighten up a little bit.

That was just one of the ways Chelsea Allen seemed to be good for him. She was helping him realize he needed to get out of his own way, out of his head—that he needed to live a little. Hell, she was making him want to do a lot of things he thought he'd never want to do again.

City Hall was located on the south side of Celebration Central Park. Across the lush expanse of green grass, he saw that a group of food trucks had gathered in the public parking lot.

"Are you hungry?" he asked.

"I'm always hungry," she said.

"Those food trucks over there are new to the area, but they have been getting rave reviews. I've always wanted to try them. Are you game?"

"I didn't bring my purse," she said. "Maybe another time?"

"Carpe diem," he said. "My treat."

Who said he wasn't spontaneous? He wasn't even irritated with Lucy anymore for calling him that. Sometimes the best cure was for someone to hold up a mirror so a person could see himself more clearly.

After his divorce he had allowed inertia to set in. He would own that. But things were changing now. Life was opening up.

He smiled at Chelsea. For the first time in a long

time he wanted to step out of the box he'd been living in for the past five years.

They walked over to the food trucks, arms bumping, hands brushing occasionally. They laughed and talked about everything and nothing in particular as they sat on a park bench eating pulled pork and cinnamon doughnuts. It was nice just to be.

"Do your parents live in London?" he asked.

She dabbed at the corners of her mouth with a napkin. "Just outside the city in a place called Longbridge. But they travel a lot."

"You have what—three siblings, if I remember correctly?"

"Two brothers and a sister. All of them older."

"What do they do?"

She frowned for a moment. "Um… My sister works in fashion. One brother is a doctor—he's quite brilliant. The other is a…bureaucrat."

"So you're the one who should know how to work the system and all its red tape," he said. "Since you have a bureaucrat in the family."

"I don't know about that. British and US zoning isn't exactly apples to apples."

"True. Are your parents retired? You mentioned that they travel a lot."

She laughed. "Why are you grilling me?"

"I'm not. I just want to know you better. I want to unravel all the mysteries of Chelsea Allen."

"I don't quite know what to say."

"I do. Chelsea Allen, you are an enigma."

"Why do you say that?"

"Because it seems like there is a whole lot about you I still don't know."

Ethan shrugged and she smiled. Once again the image of an angel came to mind. But he knew angels didn't kiss like that and they didn't have curves that tempted him to touch her in a way that was anything but innocent.

No, Chelsea Allen was no guardian angel, but that didn't stop him from wanting to believe that she might be the one who could save him from himself. She might be the one who could pull him out of this rut he'd dug for himself over the past five years and start living again.

"You know what I want to do?" she said.

"What do you want to do?"

"I want to go swing on that swing set over there. I haven't done that since I was a kid."

"Let's do it."

They got up and started making their way across the green, manicured lawn toward the empty playground.

She turned to him as they were walking. "I told you about me. Now it's your turn. Tell me about you."

"What do you want to know?"

"Everything."

Their gazes snared for an electric moment and the corner of his mouth quirked up, revealing a dimple in his left cheek. It was a little mesmerizing. She realized even if she didn't do much while she was staying in Celebration, Texas, she could pass the time looking at his dimple and be a very happy woman.

*It's the little things in life.*

"I've been divorced for five years. I was a mess for about three years after we split up, but I'm sober now."

They sat on adjacent swings but angled themselves toward each other.

"When did you become friends?" Chelsea asked. "Saturday at the wedding, you mentioned that you and Molly are good friends now."

"Actually, we are so much better as friends than lovers and especially better at friendship than being married. We just didn't want the same things in life, but we didn't realize it until after we'd tied the knot. Things between us didn't smooth out until after I sobered up."

She didn't quite know what to say. He was very forthright about his struggle, but she wanted him to take the lead in pressing further. So she walked the swing back and pushed off, pumping her legs to start the swinging momentum. It would give him an easy out if he wanted to move away from the subject.

She was surprised and glad when he continued.

"My drinking started getting out of hand when we moved to Chicago. We both traveled a lot for our jobs."

"You mentioned that she was in pharmaceutical sales, but what did you do?"

"I worked for an agricultural company in feed sales. Not very exciting, but I had a huge northwestern territory. Like I said, it involved a lot of traveling."

He got up and stood behind her, grabbing her around the waist. It was nice to feel his hands on her and she was a little disappointed when he gave her a gentle push. She stopped pumping her legs. She didn't want to go too high because she wanted to hear every word that he was confiding.

"When I was on the road I would have a couple or three beers every night—sometimes four or five. When I was home and Molly was away, I would meet up with friends every night for drinks. When she was home and we were together we would drink. There was a lot of booze involved. I was holding a lot of anger and resentment inside and that's how I numbed it. I hated living in Chicago, but I did it for her because it made her happy."

They continued that touch-push rhythm as they talked. Each time his hands were on her back, a shiver of awareness shimmied through her.

She didn't want it to stop there. She wanted to kiss him again to see if it really was as good as it had been at the wedding. Would she see sparks again?

"I don't see you as a big city kind of guy."

"I'm not, and moving away from Celebration wasn't the life plan that Molly and I originally made when we got engaged. We'd been sweethearts since high school and we'd always talked about a future together. We'd planned on going to college together. Then we were supposed to come back to Celebration and I was going to work with my dad and eventually take over the ranch after he retired. She went to business school and was supposed to keep the books and manage the business end. We'd talked about raising our kids here and living happily-ever-after. I'll bet that sounds pretty boring to someone who grew up in a place like London."

She adjusted her grip on the swing's chain, tipping her head back to look at him as she swung out. "No, not really. It's nice here. I can breathe and hear myself think."

"Yeah, but it'll get old after a while. Trust me."

"Are you over this place?" she asked.

"Me? No. I'm so deeply rooted here I can't see myself living anywhere else. Wouldn't mind traveling now and again, but this is home. Molly thought she wanted it, too. She thought that marriage and kids and family would be enough. But how could she know what she wanted when she didn't even know herself?"

"People change, I guess," Chelsea said, slowing down to a stop. "Do you think you'll ever get married again?"

"Marriage is hard. It's not the fairy tale people make it out to be. We're all human. We screw up. We make mistakes and sometimes we end up wanting different things than we thought we wanted. That's growing as a person. I get that. If you don't grow you're stagnant and that comes with its own set of tests. The challenge is when you're married and you change in opposite directions. One day you wake up and realize you love someone, but never really knew that person."

"Did you just wake up one day and decide you didn't want to live in Chicago anymore?"

"The path wasn't that direct. We'd been in Chicago a couple of years when my folks were in an accident that killed my dad and left my mom in a wheelchair. Lucy was only fourteen. Molly and I left our jobs and came home to take care of everyone and the ranch. Molly was really good to Lucy and Mom, but I knew that wasn't where she wanted to be. Then Mom died less than a year later."

Chelsea dragged her feet, stopped the swing and turned to him.

"I'm so sorry."

He gave a one-shoulder shrug. She understood, because what was there to say?

"Did Molly go back to Chicago?"

He nodded. "We'd only planned on staying until we could get Mom to the point where she was taking care of herself. She still had use of her arms and she could get around in a wheelchair. Molly kept saying that we needed to give her as much independence as possible. She was right. No grown woman wants to be treated like an invalid. But Lucy was so young and Mom never fully recovered."

With the palm of his hand, he thumped his chest in the area of his heart. "She was never the same after Dad was gone. Lucy swears she died of a broken heart."

"It sounds like it."

"After she was gone, I couldn't leave Lucy—she'd just turned fifteen. She'd just started high school and both of her parents were gone. Jude took off to ride bulls. Frankly, I wanted to stay and run the ranch. It was selfish, but it was the truth. It was the only piece of normal I could grab. I wanted to make sure my little sister was okay and I needed to make sense of things. They offered Molly her old job back in Chicago. The short version is we tried living apart for about a year and a half before we knew it wouldn't work and then we decided to split. There's a three-year period tacked on the end that's a little fuzzy and involves me nearly losing the ranch—you wouldn't have liked me then. That's why I got sober and haven't had a drink for the past two years and that brings us to now."

Tears welled in Chelsea's eyes. She was speechless.

Ethan Campbell was a good man. He was strong and solid and kind. Sure, he was a little short on patience, but he battled his demons like a gladiator. He was the kind of guy who sacrificed and didn't go all bitter martyr on everyone. He looked out for his family and neighbors and the community. He was even friends with his ex.

Here he was sharing his deep-hearted truth, but she'd only glossed over the surface of her life, which seemed so shallow by comparison. What was she supposed to tell him? *I've dated a lot of men. The one I got serious about proved I'm a poor judge of character. When my parents discovered our sex tape was all over the internet, they told me they didn't want to see my face again until I'd cleaned up the dirty mess. And, oh, yeah, Chelsea Allen isn't even my real name.*

That was rich. It was her life in a nutshell.

Would Ethan be as magnanimous toward her if

she dug deeper and told him the whole sordid truth of what brought her here? Judging by what she knew of him, he might be.

Still, right now things were so good and he looked at her like she was some kind of goddess. She couldn't bear the thought of him looking at her any other way—like she was tainted and dirty and done.

She would be leaving Celebration as soon as she'd put her life back together. In the meantime, Ethan Campbell made her want to be a better person. Was it so bad that she wanted to try to live up to that standard? Was it so wrong to want a fresh start without the permanent stain of her past fouling the future?

"I guess fate has a funny way of stepping in." She stood up and turned to face him. "Do you believe in fate, Ethan?"

"I don't know. Maybe."

The next thing she knew, Ethan's arms were around her waist, pulling her close. His lips were skimming her cheek. His eyes were an unfathomably dark shade of blue, like blue suede or a dusky sky, and they were full of desire.

Her heart hammered against her breastbone.

She wasn't sure who moved first, but it didn't matter. The world went away as his lips met hers and her hands fisted into his shirt collar, pulling him closer.

This time it was different than when they'd come together under the mistletoe. It felt all at once brandnew and like coming home. He tasted like hope and heartbreak, but it was over before it had a chance to blossom into more.

So how was it that in the span of maybe ten heart-beats a lifetime of possibilities flashed through her mind in living color so vivid they imprinted there?

This could be good.

How could this be so good and the timing so bad? Of course, she could make the bad go away. All she needed to do was tell him the truth about who she was and why she was here. But if she told him the truth, he might just get up and walk away.

Better now than later, she told herself. But some-how the pep talk didn't ring true.

He'd rested his forehead against hers. A shadow swept across his features but it didn't hide his de-sire. She breathed in his smell that was becoming so familiar—soap and leather, the citrusy scent of his aftershave—all male and intoxicating and so very arousing. Desire, heady and irresistible, engulfed her. She tried to ignore the contrast of clean male juxta-posed with the texture of his work-worn hands as he caressed the back of her neck. It was heavenly.

His mouth tempted her again and she leaned in for another taste, a taste that awakened a voracious hunger inside her. As long as they were kissing, they didn't have to talk, and if they didn't talk, she didn't have to tell him the truth.

At least not yet.

His lips parted and he deepened the kiss. Chelsea wanted to consume him. She wanted their bodies to succumb to this intense heat and meld into one.

But all too soon they returned to earth, landing with a thud. She tried to assess how he was feeling. She bit her bottom lip, gaping at him. His blue eyes seemed to be amazed and even darker—almost pitch—with wanting. Or maybe she only imagined his desire because she wanted him to feel the same things she was feeling, to have been as affected by the kiss as profoundly as she had been.

Since Hadden betrayed her, she thought no one would ever be able to break through the wall that she'd built around her heart. A wall designed to keep people out so they never got the chance to betray her the way he had.

"Should I apologize for that?" he murmured, his hand still in her hair, their foreheads still touching, her lips still tingling and craving more.

"No," she said.

"Good. Because I'm not sorry."

"Then definitely don't apologize. Because I'm not mad about it at all."

She bit her bottom lip. "Well, actually, I was quite mad about that kiss. But not in an angry way. More like a crazy about it kind of mad. So don't hesitate to do it again."

Chelsea climbed up the ladder to sweep the cobwebs off the barn's rafters. She'd attached an old towel that Juliette had bequeathed to the cause to a long-handled paint roller and voilà! Instant cobswabber.

The height of the ladder coupled with the extension of the wooden handle gave her extraordinary reach, all the way up to where the high walls connected with the roof.

The barn hadn't been occupied in ages. From the looks of it, it was entirely possible that these nether regions had never been cleared of cobwebs—even when the place had been in use. But the wood had to be cleaned before they could paint.

The guy they'd hired to help clean up had needed to leave before he finished the job so he could make it to his son's lacrosse game. He'd offered to stay, but Chelsea had sent him on with good wishes to his son for a winning game.

Chelsea didn't mind. Since they were paying him hourly, she would save Lucy a bit of money by finishing up the chores herself. Juliette was out of town on a job for the weekend. Chelsea had run home, fixed a quick bite to eat and let out Franklin before returning to the job site. A designer's duties usually didn't entail custodial services, but she didn't mind. It was nice to keep busy.

Juliette's house was lovely and warm and comfortable, but Chelsea had felt restless and cooped up. Better to expend her anxious energy on something productive rather than drive herself and the dog crazy by pacing about the place. This point was driven home when Franklin had tried to herd her toward the couch when she was pacing. If she was irritating the corgi, she knew she needed to get out and do something productive. So she'd come back to the barn. Plus, there was a better chance that she might run into Ethan at the barn than sitting on the couch watching the telly with the dog.

She hadn't seen him since yesterday when he'd brought her back to Juliette's after the park. It was clear that they were both a little confused about what to do next.

He'd excused himself, saying he needed to get back to the ranch to do his rounds. She'd welcomed the distance because she needed to put things into perspective.

She could still feel the power of his kiss on her lips. The lingering effects shot an arrow straight down to her lady parts, and they were begging her to get to know Ethan Campbell much better.

After she had a chance to step back and give her ovaries a chance to calm down, common sense stepped in and reminded her that it wasn't a smart time to lose her wits over a handsome cowboy.

But her ovaries begged to differ. To hell with what she *should* and *shouldn't* do. She was attracted to him. He was attracted to her. They were consenting adults. What was wrong with having a little fling while she was here? She'd said she wouldn't allow Hadden to cast her in the role of victim. What better way to break out of that corral than to ride that cowboy until all her troubles fell away?

*And where would you like him to send the souvenir recording?*

*Bloody hell! Decent people didn't do things like that.*

Ethan was friends with his ex-wife. He hadn't

sought revenge. He wasn't inclined to slut-shame her because she hurt his feelings.

She remembered a saying in a needlepoint picture hanging up in Juliette's house: *I'm a grown-ass lady and I do what I want.*

So there. She would do what she wanted.

For now she took a moment to survey the structure from her high perch. Already, they had a long, hard row to hoe if they were going to get the place ready for Connor Bryce's party. Actually, she was going to suggest that they have a grand opening party before Connor and his fiancée's wedding reception so that they could work out any kinks.

She hoped the subcontractors would be conscientious about showing up on the promised dates and times. Ethan had said they would and that their work was of exceptionally good quality. Probably one of the perks of living in a small town like Celebration, Texas, and knowing the people you hired. If they didn't deliver what they promised when they promised, the person who'd hired them knew where they lived.

They'd know soon enough, once the plans were approved and the real work started.

She couldn't imagine such service in London. Even though this was her first job as head designer—er, okay, so she was the *only* designer on this project and she was donating her services—the process seemed a far cry from the horror stories she'd heard at Hargraves.

Of course, as a newbie, she'd never been allowed

to roll up her sleeves and run with a project. Her days were filled with important tasks such as sorting fabric samples and culling through product lists, identifying and deleting discontinued items and searching for suitable replacements.

In the short time she was with the firm, Geoffrey Hargraves had allowed her to choose three light fixtures for a movie star's London flat. The client got to pick her favorite. Chelsea had never learned which one the client chose—nor had she known the identity of said movie star because of the firm's steadfast rule that a client's privacy was to be protected above all else. She knew better than to ask and Geoffrey certainly didn't volunteer the information. So that was the extent of the creative input she'd been allowed to give during her few weeks at the firm. Then the scandal had broken and she'd gotten the boot before she had a chance to prove herself.

There was something strangely fulfilling about conceiving an idea in her imagination and knowing she could watch it take shape right before her eyes.

She hoped Lucy would find a similar feeling of accomplishment once her business began gaining momentum.

Lost in thought, Chelsea swiped the long-handled dust mop as far as she could reach across the slanted ceiling. How ironic it was that she'd been searching for herself in London's hubbub and it had never seemed to fit. *She* had never felt like she fit, despite the fact that London, with all its posh parties, was home and its fancy people were her people. But they weren't really. It had always felt so superficial, but she hadn't realized the shallowness had been the root of her discontent. She hadn't known it until she'd gotten away from it and had been forced to face herself in the quiet.

Who knew she'd be more content alone on a Friday night cleaning a barn than clubbing in Ibiza? Even more of a shock was who knew she'd connect with herself in a place like Celebration, Texas?

London had been the puzzle piece that looked as if it *should* fit, but didn't quite match up. No one would've ever known it really didn't belong until the rest of the pieces were set in place and the picture was off and a piece was missing elsewhere. Celebration seemed a good fit for the puzzle that was her life. At least for the time being she could catch her breath and get in touch with her heart. And maybe get to know Ethan Campbell a little better.

The squeak of the barn door opening startled her out of her reverie. She flinched and lost her grip on the wooden pole and it fell from her hand, landing with a clattering thud at Ethan's feet.

Chelsea's heart thudded and the butterflies that had been her constant companion since she'd arrived swooped in formation.

"Good grief, Ethan! Don't sneak up on me like that."

Bloody hell, and she'd let the accent slip.

He held up his hands surrender-style, but her accent didn't seem to have registered with him. "Don't fall off the ladder. I didn't intend to sneak. I had no idea you were in here. What are you doing here this late?"

Her heart was still thudding and she placed a hand on her chest as if that would help it settle down.

"I'm working," she said. "Kenny French needed to leave for his son's sporting event. He wasn't finished with the cobweb dusting and I thought I would wrap it up for him. It will save Lucy some money. For that matter, why are you here?"

*Thank God you're here.*

"I'm sorry I scared you. I was driving home and I saw the light on and came in to turn it off."

She laughed and loosened her death grip on the side of the ladder. "Please don't leave me alone in the dark."

Her lips tingled as she thought of yesterday's kiss, the feel of his lips on hers, his strong, capable hands on her body and how she'd hated it when he'd said good-night. What would it be like to be alone in the dark with Ethan? Her heart rate kicked up again and a slow burn of approval started deep in her belly. What would he do if she climbed down from the ladder and proceeded to jump his bones?

"I wouldn't dream of it," he said.

"I beg your pardon?"

"I wouldn't leave you in the dark. Not alone, anyway."

Ethan bent down and picked up her dust mop. From her perch on the ladder, she could see that grit and dust from the floor now stuck to the cobwebs.

If she kept using it, she would scatter dirt and dust all over and make the mess worse.

"You're going to need a clean towel," Ethan said.

She frowned and started down the ladder. "Or I could simply rinse off that one."

"There's no water out here. They won't have it turned on until next week after we get the permits."

"Does Lucy have a spigot outside her house?" Chelsea asked.

"Speaking of, where is my sister and why isn't she out here helping you? Again."

With both feet now planted firmly on the ground Chelsea stepped away from the ladder.

"She had another business meeting tonight. I don't mind working by myself. The quiet is kind of nice."

Ethan studied her in that unapologetic way of his. The man was such a study of contradictions. On one hand he was gruff and a little rough around the edges, but on the other, he was so comfortable in his own skin, so completely unselfconscious. A refreshing change from the guys she was used to. Ethan Campbell, all long, tall, six-foot-something of him, was a take-me-as-I-am-or-leave-me-the-hell-alone kind of guy. Chelsea had to smile to herself because she was ever so tempted to take him exactly as he was right here, right now.

"You don't strike me as the type who thrives in solitude," he said.

How on earth had he come to that conclusion? "Why would you think that?"

The dimple in his left cheek winked at her again. He was flirting with her. Her heart soared.

"I can usually get a pretty good read on people."

"Is that so?" she said, trying to play it cool.

He nodded.

Swallowing the urge to come clean and confess everything to him, she put her hands on her hips and tilted her head to one side. "Tell me, what else do you think you know about me?"

She'd learned a long time ago not to give anything away. If he'd learned something, say, about the video, let him broach the subject first. If he knew anything. And she was betting that he didn't. Praying that he didn't.

*God, please don't let him know.*

He studied her for a moment and her heart thudded with each passing second.

"I think you're one hell of a hard worker and I think you look like you could use a break. Want to come to my place and have something to drink?"

She started to protest, but he stopped her.

"Come on. It's Friday night and the two of us are standing here in an old barn. We can do better than this."

She always had been a sucker for dimples. His dimples in particular.

"Well, since you put it that way. How can I refuse?"

After she stepped outside, he clicked off the light and shut the door. The night air was springtime cool, and she caught a whiff of something heady and wonderful perfuming the air.

"What is that lovely scent?" she asked, lifting her face into the evening breeze.

"That's jasmine. It grows hardy out here. That's it over there, climbing the fence."

"Mmm. I could bathe in it. It's intoxicating."

He followed her to the passenger side of his truck, opened the door for her and held her elbow, helping her into the Ford's cabin. When she turned to thank him she saw him draw in a deep breath.

"Funny how you can get so used to something you don't even notice it anymore," he said. "It is nice."

They made small talk as they followed a dirt road that was bordered by white post and rail horse fencing on either side. The path cut through a large stretch of grassy land. It led to a ranch-style house that sat a good distance off the highway.

The amber porch light welcomed them and illuminated two rocking chairs and several barrel planters brimming over with an assortment of colorful flowers.

"Is this your house?" she asked as she climbed the steps.

He nodded.

She couldn't recall the mental picture that had come to mind when she'd pictured Ethan at home, but it hadn't been quite like this.

"It's nice," she said as she stood on the porch, squinting out through the veil of inky evening, trying to get the lay of the land. There was a lot of it, for as far as she could see.

Some kind of night creature chirped in the distance. "Does all this property belong to you?"

"Lucy, our brother Jude and I each own a third." He turned the knob on the unlocked door. They stepped inside. "We decided it would be easier to split it into three equal parcels. Lucy owns the area surrounding the barn. This part is mine. Jude owns the property over on the west side. We each inherited about three hundred acres."

"That's a lot to take care of." She glanced around as she followed him into the living room. The eighties-era decor was rustic, but the house seemed neat and tidy. Chelsea imagined that it probably looked exactly as it had when Ethan was growing up. Since his parents were gone he probably found some comfort in that.

"It keeps me busy," Ethan said. "I have my routine. As long as I stick to it, upkeep's not a problem. I like keeping busy."

"You and I have that in common," she said. "We both like to keep busy."

He cocked a brow, as if he might have read something into her words. But then he nodded and gestured to the couch. "Make yourself comfortable. Would you like something to drink?"

"A glass of wine?" Her hand flew to her mouth. The words had no sooner escaped her lips when she realized what she said and that he probably didn't keep alcohol in the house.

She waved her hand as if to erase her mistake. "Actually, water is fine. I'm sorry, Ethan. I didn't mean to be insensitive."

He shook his head. "You don't need to apologize. I wish I could offer you wine, but I don't have any. We could go to Murphy's Pub if you want. They have a good wine list."

"I don't need wine. I'm sorry. I shouldn't have—"

"You don't have to tiptoe around the subject when you're with me. You're not the one who has a problem with alcohol. You can have wine when you're with me and you don't have to apologize for it."

She thought about the people she used to go out and about with in London. The parties, the mornings when she would sleep until noon because she was nursing a headache from overindulging the night before. She'd never thought she'd abused alcohol. Not even after Hadden recorded their intimacy unbeknownst to her. Maybe if she had been more cognizant it wouldn't have happened.

It certainly wouldn't hurt her to abstain for a while.

"How about some coffee?" she asked.

"Coming right up."

She followed him into the kitchen, which also looked like it had been frozen in all of its eighties grandeur, with its ivory-painted cabinets, sky blue tile backsplash, butcher-block countertops and light blue-and-yellow linoleum floor.

Just like the living room, it was neat and clean. Everything seemed to be freshly scrubbed and in its place. An honest kitchen for an honest man. Just like Ethan, it was unapologetically bona fide. No arrogance. No pretense. No airs. It was what it was and there was beauty in that.

As she watched him spoon coffee into a filter, the old familiar tangle of anger at Hadden and self-loathing for landing herself in this degrading situation knotted in her stomach. She felt like such a fraud standing in Ethan's house, pretending to be someone she wasn't, someone virtuous and honorable. The person he deserved didn't hide her name or her reason for being here. She certainly didn't fake an American accent for fear that she would be found out for who she really was.

Again, the sudden need to confess everything to him swept through her with gale-force intensity.

What would he think of her if he knew her real story?

What would this man, who took pride in carrying on his family's legacy and fiercely protected his little sister, think of her if he knew the truth?

What would he think of her if he saw the recording?

The humiliation of disgrace bloomed on her cheeks as he turned around to say something to her.

"Are you okay?" he asked.

*No.*

"I'm fine." She mustered her best lying smile. "Why would you think I wasn't?"

He watched her for a minute.

Maybe she wasn't as good at deception as she thought.

"You looked upset. Are you— Is this okay? If you're uncomfortable—"

The coffeemaker started hissing and chugging.

"I'm not uncomfortable," she said, hanging tight to her enunciated American accent. She just couldn't seem to let go of it. "I promise."

Her last words were softer. Because she really was okay being here with him. No, more than okay. She wanted to be here. That part wasn't a lie. She just wished it all could be aboveboard.

She wanted to kiss Ethan again. In full self-disclosure, she wanted to do more than kiss him. She hadn't felt that way about a man in a long time. Ethan Campbell was built from different stock than Hadden Hastings.

But she was getting ahead of herself. Right now they were having coffee. It was a chance to get to know a man who seemed to be interested in her for herself. Not because of her brother's political connections or because her sister could score front-row seats at any number of fashion week shows.

His lopsided grin brought his dimple out to play. "Good, because I'm glad you're here."

Chelsea experienced a moment of clarity. This was how it should be between a man and a woman. Organic attraction. Nothing premeditated or conditional. With Ethan, she could glimpse the potential to becoming the person she always wanted to be. This person she was pretending to be now.

This was nice…and intimate.

"So, I never asked. How long are you staying? It seems a shame that Juliette has to be away so much of the time you're here."

"It's sort of open-ended right now."

He looked a little surprised. "Are you on vacation or between jobs?"

"It's a long story," she said.

"I have all night," he returned.

That deep Texas drawl wound its way down her spine like a velvet caress and sent a shiver that reached all the way to her core. That was a loaded statement, and there was that inflection in his voice that she could take all sorts of different ways.

"What a coincidence. So do I."

## Chapter Nine

Ethan couldn't deny the spark of longing that surged through him. He wanted her. He hadn't wanted a woman like this for a very long time.

There had been other women since Molly. Most of them had been one-nighters, especially before he'd gotten a handle on the drinking. But since he'd been sober, the idea of sex for sex's sake didn't appeal to him as much. Sure, he still had needs, but sex to numb, sex to forget himself for a while, just didn't seem worth the hustle anymore. Living in a small town like Celebration, it wasn't really feasible to sleep with your neighbor or the bartender at Bistro Saint-Germain and expect to remain platonically friendly. Word got around. Women started comparing notes.

Things felt different with Chelsea. It wasn't just

because she was leaving soon. At first he thought it might be convenient, but she was Juliette's best friend. Juliette had always been like family, even though she wasn't seeing his brother, Jude, anymore. By virtue of friendship, it took Chelsea out of the one-nighter category.

So, where did that leave them?

Chelsea was the first woman in a very long time who had thawed his frozen heart and warmed him to the idea of something more than casual sex, something more than friendship.

They had taken their coffee into the living room and were sitting comfortably close on the couch. They'd talked about the barn; they'd talked about horses and going riding sometime this week; they'd even talked about the weather. It wasn't that they'd run out of things to say as much as it was that with each exhausted topic, the urge to kiss her, to touch her, to pick her up and take her to his bed, edged out his ability to keep up a conversation.

But he didn't want her to feel like he'd brought her here with ulterior motives.

His eyes fell to the creamy expanse of her neck, which looked enticing and smooth beneath the V of her T-shirt. He forced his gaze back up to meet hers.

Finally, she reached out and took his cup and set it on the coffee table. "Would you stop being such a gentleman and kiss me?"

That was all it took.

She melted into him. He bent his head, and as if she sensed the subtle movement, she tilted her head up and met his lips. The feel of her in his arms—the way she fit so perfectly—reminded him of when he'd kissed her at the park. They hadn't spoken of that kiss. He thought he'd be just fine with that, but the minute he'd walked in and saw her on that ladder tonight, he knew he wanted to kiss her again. No, not just kiss her, he wanted to make love to her. Judging from the way she was holding on to him, she didn't seem to mind venturing out of the friend zone, either.

Her body, so close and supple, made him yearn to explore her swells and valleys. His hands got a head start on doing just that. He kissed her gently at first then more insistently as he pulled her flush against him.

"You are so beautiful," he said, trailing a finger down her jawline. Then his lips followed the path his finger had traced.

She sighed. It was almost inaudible, but he felt it when he found her lips again. He tightened the embrace in response; his hands swept down her back, over the slight rectangle of bare skin where her cotton shirt met the waistband of her low-slung jeans.

As they deepened the kiss, his tongue swirling around hers, her response was so invitingly erotic that he didn't even realize the rasping moan echoing in his head had escaped from his own throat.

He pulled back, trying to read her, needing to make sure she wanted this as much as he did. If she didn't, he would honor that, but they needed to stop now. He needed to take her back to Juliette's and they needed to say good-night.

"Are you okay with this?" he asked.

"I'm more than okay." She looped her arms around his neck and brushed a feather-light kiss on his lips. "Ethan, I have a feeling we're both going to be even better very soon."

When she covered his mouth with hers, it was all he needed to extinguish any doubts that she wanted him as badly as he wanted her. He longed to show her exactly how hot he burned for her.

He took possession of her body, craving the feel of her hands in his hair; the searing heat of her touch on his shoulders, trailing down his back; the white-hot ecstasy of skin on bare skin as she slid her hands underneath his shirt. They held each other so close he could barely breathe. But her kiss was the only air he needed. She breathed life into him, imbued him with something he hadn't felt in a very long time. Something he'd been missing. He was finding it in a woman who was getting under his skin as deftly as she crawled in through bathroom windows. Breaking and entering.

Breaking down his barriers and entering his heart.

Even if it would be temporary.

Right now he had to have her. He couldn't get enough of her. Just like earlier when he'd had a hard time finding the words to explain what he wanted, how he felt. She'd met him halfway, bridged that gap. Now all he could do was show her how he felt.

With Chelsea in his arms, the heaviness he had been carrying around was lifted off his shoulders and out of his heart. He held her close, afraid that if he turned her loose, she might slip away. He kissed her more urgently this time, taking possession of her mouth, craving the shared heat.

Her skin was smooth and her body was firm with a sexy, feminine strength that had him summoning every ounce of self-control to keep from taking her right then and there.

"Let's go into the bedroom," she murmured, as if reading his mind.

He kissed her deeply as he backed her down the hall—tongues thrusting, hands fighting with buttons, teeth nipping gently at tender skin.

Their ravenous slow two-step finally landed them in his bedroom.

Need guided his hands as he explored the swell of her breasts and skimmed her belly until he found the tail of her T-shirt and slid his hand underneath. When his hands found her breasts again, she drew in a ragged breath. As he moved his thumb over her nipple, hard as a rock even through her lacy bra, a low moan escaped her lips and he nearly came undone.

She was spellbound by his touch. He pulled her shirt over her head, and got rid of her bra, jeans and panties.

"Where is it?" he murmured, brow arched in a way that was so sexy it nearly made her come undone.

"Where is what?" she answered in her most playful voice.

"That tattoo." He ran his hands down the side of her and slid them underneath her so that he cupped her bottom with his hands, pulling her close. She could feel his arousal.

She smiled up at him. "What makes you think I have a tattoo?"

"I gathered as much from that conversation about tattoos we had at the wedding. You made a pretty good argument that even classy women have them, and you're probably the classiest woman I've ever met. Ever since then, I've been trying to imagine where a classy woman hides her wild tattoo?"

Chelsea's breath hitched in her throat. Oh, no. He knew. If they were going to make love, if this was really going to happen she should tell him everything right now, before they went any further.

"On her wild side, of course." Chelsea wriggled out of his embrace and turned around to show him the spiral of Sanskrit words tattooed on the right side of her derriere. "It means, *live with no regrets— contentedness is the only path to happiness.*"

A low, sexy growl that sounded like approval escaped his throat. He moistened his lips with his tongue and kissed her again. Even though this relationship, this fling—whatever it was they were doing—was temporary, she should tell him the truth. She wanted to trust him. She did. She had to or she wouldn't be able to give herself to him. She couldn't lie here with him, vulnerable, exposed, allowing him to break through her personal barricades, inviting him to partake of her body, if there wasn't mutual trust.

"Ethan, I need to explain something—"

"*Shhhh.* Not right now." He kissed her on the forehead and eased her onto the bed. "Wait right here. I'll be right back."

She watched him undress in a small shaft of moonlight that filtered in through a slim gap in the drawn drapes. The faint light illuminated the room just enough so that she could see his muscled body, the long-limbed ease of his gait as he rounded the bed, the plane of his taut stomach, the bunch of his biceps as he bent to pull something—a condom, she guessed—from the nightstand drawer. He lowered himself down onto the bed next to her, stretched out beside her and rose up on his right elbow so that he was looking at her.

"Are you okay?" He ran the pad of his thumb over her bottom lip. "Is this okay?"

She nodded.

*Say something.*

"We don't have to do this if you're uncomfortable."

"No, I'm fine."

She needed to tell him the truth, but she couldn't focus on words with Ethan's hand tracing circles on her bare stomach. She shivered, unsure if the frisson was induced by guilt or her overwhelming desire for him.

Or maybe both.

Definitely both.

As she watched him slide the condom down his considerable length, all she could think about was what that big, strong body of his would do to hers, the pleasurable heights to which he could take her. The delicious thought pushed the explanation that she'd been piecing together—the words she should be saying right now—out of her head. The clarification of who she really was—why she was in Celebration, why she'd given him a fake name—faded farther and farther into the back of her mind until all she was aware of was the hunger in his eyes and the way moonlight played off his dark brown hair. She ran her fingers through locks that curled defiantly at the nape of his neck, working her way around to push wayward strands off his forehead.

Her confession had to come right now...

But right now he was addling her with gentle caresses and soft kisses that paid homage to her body's most sensitive places—the tender and oft forgotten spot at the base of her ears, the dip where her neck gave way to her collarbone, the ticklish zone under her arm, revealed when he laced his fingers in hers and pinned her arms over her head. He trailed sweet kisses down her body until he reached the private place hidden between her thighs and his tongue found its way to her center.

He held her under his spell, captivated by pure bliss until she cried out in pleasure that was so powerful it pulsed off her in waves.

Ethan's gaze locked on hers as he settled himself between her legs and thrust gently to fill her. She gasped and raised her hips to meet him and take him all the way in. She reveled in the sensation, in the wonder of this man inside her.

They both held still for a moment as if they were afraid to break the fragile spell of their joining. She looked into his eyes—eyes that were the deepest shade of blue she'd ever seen, like India ink or a midnight sky—and she smoothed her hands down his back to cup his bum, holding him there.

"You feel even better than I imagined," he whispered before he lowered his mouth to hers for another kiss.

She pulled him closer, sinking in and savoring the deliciousness of him.

Finally, when he pulled back to look at her and she smiled up at him in a lusty daze, he began to move inside her, slower than she wanted, each movement purposeful and deliberate, promising to drive her mad.

As he thrust again, she rose up to meet him and he slipped his hands beneath her bottom and shifted her so that he could go deeper. Her body ignited with a glorious passion so intense that it flared from the inside out and only got better when he began pumping his hips a little faster.

Chelsea wrapped her legs around his hips as the golden warmth gathered in her belly and blossomed outward. Each stroke, deeper and deeper, brought her closer to release. Her body shook from need as she reveled in the sensation of his every move. Ethan steadily increased his rhythm, and his breathing was heavy and raspy against her ear.

When the pleasure wave crested, a moan escaped her lips. His mouth found hers again. Her release was suspended for a moment that seemed to stretch into eternity before finally spilling over. Ethan's kiss caught her cry of pleasure and it seemed to fuel his own.

"Chelsea," he groaned as he made his final powerful thrust.

Ethan's eyes closed and his body tensed as the orgasm shook him. Chelsea slid her hands up along the rigid muscles of his biceps and shoulders until her fingers curled into his hair. He hovered above her for a moment, breathing hard. He looked sexy as hell and quite satisfied. She tried to pull him down on top of her, but not before he kissed her again as if drawing a sustaining life's breath from the final moments of their coupling.

Finally, he collapsed next to her, turning her body so that she spooned against him. He pulled her in close with a possessive arm so that her body was flush against his.

Feeling warm and protected and utterly spent, she curled into him, basking in the heat that radiated off his skin.

Their lovemaking had zapped her energy; yet the physical closeness, the way he continued to hold her, filled her heart. Even as her body gave in to the satisfied weariness, every muscle in her body relaxed. If she could only quiet the voices in her head that nagged, *You should've told him. You need to tell him.*

She would.

Soon.

Just not right now.

## Chapter Ten

It was nice making coffee for two and bringing a cup to Chelsea in bed. Even so, Ethan hated to wake her up. Instead, he wanted to crawl back under the covers next to her and make love to her for the rest of the day, shutting out the world so it was just the two of them.

However, Ethan had awakened to a text from Tyler Jennings, the vet who looked after the Triple C's horses, saying that Calendula, a mare they were looking to breed with a stallion on Kingston Farms, was ready to go. Since they were inseminating the old-fashioned way, they'd been on standby for signs that the time was right to deliver Calendula to her stud, and the time had come.

Crawling back into bed with Chelsea sounded a hell of a lot better than delivering a horse.

His body responded, seconding the motion, but good sense reminded him he had a short window to load up Calendula and drive her over to the Kingston ranch in Burleson, about an hour southwest of Celebration. No matter how much every primal cell in him protested, Ethan knew he couldn't put off the transport or they'd have to wait another month for Calendula to complete yet another cycle.

Chelsea looked beautiful lying there with her blond hair spread all over his pillow. He set the hot coffee on the nightstand and sat down next to her on the side of the bed. As he brushed a wisp of hair off her forehead, her eyes fluttered open. She blinked a couple of times as if trying to orient herself. Then a slow smile spread over her face.

"Good morning," she said, stretching luxuriously, reminding him of a sleek, golden cat. Her voice was husky with sleep.

"Morning." He knew he was grinning like a damn fool, but he couldn't help himself.

"Is that coffee I smell?"

"I brought you a cup. Black. Just how you like it." Even though he'd just learned how she took her coffee last night, it felt intimate. Like he knew her. It seemed like he did. She felt comfortable and familiar in the best way. A way that made him hungry to learn more. He handed her the mug and she scooted up to a sitting position, modestly covering her bareness with the sheet as she accepted the cup.

"Thank you," she rasped. "Wow. Coffee in bed. I could get used to this."

So could he. He would bring her coffee every morning if it meant he could wake up next to her.

"Sorry to get you up so early," he said. "Turns out, I have to deliver a horse this morning. I didn't know about it until after the vet had done his rounds."

"Is everything okay? I hope it's not an emergency."

"Nope. Just nature calling. She's ready to be bred."

"You don't do the breeding here?" she asked.

"Sometimes," he said. "This is a special arrangement and it's easier to transport a mare than it is to wrangle and move a ton of bucking stallion. We've been on standby for days and the vet just gave me the green light that she's ready to go."

"Oh, I'm sorry. I don't want to make you late. I can leave." She held out the cup, trying to give it back to him, but he waved her off.

"No, take your time. Drink your coffee. I have some things I need to do before I leave." He stood. Before he turned to go, he added, "In fact, why don't you come with me?"

He hadn't planned on asking, but he heard the words slip past his lips before he could overthink it.

"To deliver the horse?"

He shrugged. "Yeah, it's over in Burleson. A couple hours away. It might be nice for you to see some of the countryside. We can drop off the horse and grab lunch on the way back. I can have you back here by early afternoon."

She made a noise as if the suggestion surprised her. "You know how I love horses."

Yes, he did know, and it added to what was already turning into a good situation.

"Well, then, that settles it. You have to come."

"But I'm not exactly dressed for the occasion." She glanced down and then a wicked smile tugged at the corners of her lips. "I'm not exactly dressed, period."

"And you look amazing, exactly the way you are." He leaned down and captured her mouth with his. Her lips were warm from the coffee and tasted like heaven.

She pulled back, nipping gently at his bottom lip. "I'd better pass and let you take care of business. And I need to—" He kissed her again, showing he didn't intend to take no for an answer. But she persisted, "I need to take care of business, too, over at the barn. Time is ticking if we're going to have that place in shape for the grand opening party."

"I think I know of a party that would be much more fun…" He kissed her long and slow. "And some business we could take care of together." He took the cup from her hands and stretched out next to her, finding her lips again. She responded by deepening the kiss, and for a few moments they lost themselves in each other. Until she shattered magic with one single word.

"Franklin."

"No. Um…I'm Ethan."

She laughed. "I could not be more aware of who *you* are, but I need to get back to Juliette's so I can feed the dog and let him out to take care of his own business. Poor dog is probably about ready to burst, if he hasn't already. I took him out about nine o'clock last night before I went to work at the barn. Juliette is counting on me and I'm sure he's wondering where I am."

Ethan propped himself up on his right elbow and marveled at her beauty—fresh-faced and perfect in all of her imperfections—and there weren't many. With his free hand he ran a finger down to the sexy place where her cleavage peeked out from the edge of the sheet, enticing him to unwrap her and explore the rest of her all over again. In the early morning light, he was sure she would be even better than last night. She was a natural beauty—wide-set, crystal-clear blue eyes, high cheekbones, Cupid's bow mouth, small, upturned nose made even more alluring by that spray of freckles and the way it wrinkled when she smiled. He wanted to photograph her with his mind, exactly the way she looked right now.

"That's an easy fix," he said. "I can drive you back to Juliette's and tend to the dog while you shower and get dressed. I would recommend jeans. Although, as I said, I'm particularly partial to what you're wearing now. In case you needed fashion advice."

She laughed as she swatted him away. "I can see I shouldn't take fashion advice from you. You'll get me arrested for indecent exposure. So you need to let me get out of bed. Otherwise, I might just keep you here all day."

"I didn't realize that was an option," Ethan said, tracing her jawline with the pad of his finger. "Because it is very tempting."

"No. It's not an option." She turned her head and captured his finger with her lips, giving it a playful suck. He could tell by her smile that she was fully aware that her actions were contradicting her words. "But I'll go with you and I know of a very exclusive party happening when we get back. And you're invited. So the sooner we deliver that horse…"

She pursed her lips and cocked her right brow. She looked so damn sexy it was all he could do to keep from taking her again. But from somewhere in the back of his mind the voice of reason prevailed. He inhaled a deep breath, which was supposed to help him put himself back together, but it smelled of her, of them.

The only safe bet was to remove himself from temptation and start getting the trailer hitched to the back of his truck—a most unsexy option, but nonetheless, the only option. But not before he claimed one last, long, sensual kiss.

With their lips still touching and her hands fisted into the front of his shirt, she whispered. "I can't recall ever looking so forward to a party in my entire life."

Calendula was a fine, muscular red bay Thoroughbred with black points. Chelsea stroked the mare's nose, admiring her beautiful chocolate eyes, graceful neck, and gorgeous long legs. She'd opted to stay outside with the horse as Ethan wrapped up business in the office. Being out here in the fresh air and open country, dressed casually, reminded her of how much she used to love to ride and how much she was longing to get into the saddle again.

When Ethan brought her home, Chelsea had texted Juliette and asked to borrow a cap and a casual T-shirt. Generous Juliette had given her the go-ahead to help herself to anything she needed. So Chelsea had donned the hat, threading her ponytail through the open space in the back and pulling it down onto her forehead, pairing it with sunglasses, dungarees and Tim McGraw concert T-shirt. She'd reproached herself after kissing Ethan so openly out in public the other day. While she'd gained a false sense of security in Celebration, even though it was highly unlikely that anyone would recognize her—especially dressed like this—she needed to be careful.

Still, she didn't need to make herself crazy, which is why she'd decided to spend the day out with Ethan. Lucy recognizing her had been a fluke. How many other people from the Texas hill country would recognize her in this context? She'd probably have a better chance winning the lottery than being spotted in the crowd. She wanted this time with Ethan. She wanted to be a normal person who was out with the guy she liked, doing the normal things normal couples did. No pressures to look or act a certain way and certainly not being singled out as tramp, a slut, a whore—as the woman whose most intimate moments had been broadcast for the world to see. She shook the thought from her head, determined not to let it cloud her mood.

"Can we go riding tomorrow?" she asked Ethan

after they were on the road again. "I should be at a pretty good spot to take a break by then—even after playing hooky today. It's been so long and I really miss it. There aren't many opportunities to ride in the city and it's been ages—years, in fact—since I've had time to get out to the country."

He slanted her a glance. "Sure. We can go anytime you want. Just name it. Did you have your own horse when you were growing up?"

"I did. His name was Bromley. I loved that horse like family."

"What happened to Bromley?"

"He got old and I got busy. I haven't been riding since he died."

In the distance she spied a colorful collection of neon and steel. It looked like a festival of some sort.

"What's going on up there?" she asked, happy for a valid reason to steer the subject away from Bromley and possible segues to Longbridge.

"That's the Celebration Spring Fair. It just started a couple of days ago."

"Let's stop. Can we?"

"Yes. Let's take a day off and go to the fair. Even if it's just for a few hours."

"I thought you had a tight schedule you needed to stick to?"

"I do, but that's what assistant managers are for. Let me make a call and we can make a day of it."

She felt as giddy as a child at the thought. "I've never been to a fair like this."

He laughed. "This is the best days of my youth in

one tacky, neon-lit diorama. I grew up going but it's been a few years since I last went. When I was a kid I used to raise livestock to show through 4-H."

"I wish I could've seen you as a little boy. I'll bet you were adorable."

He parked the truck and made his calls and the next thing she knew, they were in the thick of things.

The air buzzed with the faint sound of music from a country concert happening on the other side of the fairgrounds. Chelsea didn't recognize the tune because it was muffled by the sounds of the generators that powered the rides and the screams and laughs of the revelers who seemed to be having the time of their lives. The sum total created such a festive atmosphere Chelsea couldn't help but smile.

The air was heavy with the smell of livestock, diesel fuel and a mélange of food aromas wafting from the various vendors on the crowded midway.

Chelsea had never seen anything like the food offered for sale: spaghetti and meatballs on a stick, pizza cones, deep-fried Twinkies and candy bars, frozen, chocolate-covered Key lime pie. There was even a stall featuring chicken-fried bacon.

"Do you want to grab some lunch?" he asked.

"Here?" she said.

"Of course. Who doesn't love fair food?"

"I don't know. I've never had fair food, but I think I've gained five pounds simply smelling it. I don't suppose they'd have a salad stand, would they?" She was joking about the salad, of course, but not about never having tried fair food. And part of her—the part that was tired of trying to conform to the standards her family and the media had set for her, the part of her that had been trying to please everyone but herself—wanted to take a bite of every single unhealthy, nutrient-void junk food delicacy. Maybe even two bites. Especially the more traditional carnival fare that Ethan was pointing out now—the funnel cakes and French fries and corn dogs and gossamer-pink cotton candy. Especially the cotton candy.

"You've never had fair food?"

She shook her head. "I told you, I've never been to one of these things."

"That explains why you don't know that vegetables—unless they're fried or buttered corn on the cob—are against the law at a county fair. I think it's a capital offense."

He narrowed his eyes. "I can't believe you've never been to the fair."

She shrugged and shook her head again. "In the UK we have livestock shows, but I've never had the opportunity to attend."

"Never had the opportunity, huh?" His mouth quirked up on one side. "In other words, this really isn't your gig?"

"Hey, I was the one who suggested we stop. Don't try to make me out to be some sort of snob."

"You? A snob? Heavens, no. And since you're in such an adventurous mood, I'll get a wide sampling." He gestured toward the food stalls. "That way you can have the authentic Texas county fair experience."

True to his word, he purchased a lot of food. It

bordered on being obscene. But it was glorious. They found a picnic table in the shade and took their time eating. There was so much food and it was all so delicious that she thought he was going to have to carry her out of there, but after they'd finished, Ethan grabbed her hand and pulled her to her feet.

"Let's go walk it off," he said. "I've introduced you to my favorite foods, now I want you to meet my favorite rides." He laced his fingers through hers as they walked the midway.

He held her hand so unselfconsciously that she couldn't give in to her own uncertainty—the thought of being openly affectionate in public…again…with this man…in this new…this…romance? Affair? Whatever it was that they were doing… It made her insides zing in a little cha-cha. She closed her fingers around his rather than pulling away. Since she was throwing caution to the wind, she decided she wouldn't even stop him if he tried to kiss her. In fact, she kind of wanted him to kiss her, right here, right now. Because the only thing that seemed more delicious than all the food at the fair was Ethan's lips.

Really, what was the worst thing that could happen if they kissed right here out in the open? They might draw attention to themselves and someone might recognize her. In that cap and behind those glasses?

Fat chance.

People might look at them in a get-a-room way, but out here no one cared if they kissed. Out here they were nobodies. She was a nobody. Anonymous.

Un-newsworthy. And she couldn't remember the last time she'd felt so free.

In that instant she realized she had a choice: she could either hide away and let Hadden win or she could take back her life. Have fun for the first time in a long time with a man who made her think and feel things she hadn't felt in a long time.

She chose to ignore the little voice that nudged her—if she wanted this to work with Ethan, she knew she had to tell him the truth.

But not right now.

Right now the sun was shining and the gentle breeze was blowing and the warmth of Ethan's hand in hers made the late-spring morning almost perfect. She hadn't been this happy in ages. There was a chance that he might pull away, might be angry with her for not telling him the truth before now—or he might not want to associate with a woman with a past. He might not want any part of…*this*…of them…after she told him the real reason she'd come to Celebration.

So, right now all she wanted was this day. She knew she was being selfish, but she was going to enjoy herself being a woman who was falling for a man.

Tonight.

She would tell him tonight. In the meantime she held Ethan's hand as they walked down the midway. She hugged him when he won her a bear by throwing a ball and knocking over a triangle of bottles. They rode the rides, shared some cotton candy and she didn't balk when he stopped at a booth that was selling kisses for two dollars each to raise money for disabled veterans. Ethan slapped down a ten-dollar bill.

Only, Ethan didn't collect five kisses from the cute redhead who was working the booth. He turned and gathered Chelsea in his arms, tipped her backward and planted a toe-curling kiss on her mouth right there in front of God and everyone who cared to watch.

When they finally came up for air, he said, "That should count as five kisses, shouldn't it? I wouldn't want to waste your time with piddlin' pecks on the lips."

Then, without another word, he swept her off to the Ferris wheel. He put his arm around her, and they sat in silence, the big bear he'd won for her at their feet as the ride carried them up, up, up above Buxton County. He pointed out Celebration to the north and Burleson, where they'd just delivered the horse, behind them.

People would eventually get bored with the video. Their interest would shift when something fresh and more exciting came along. Even though it made Chelsea feel like a freak in a circus sideshow, she clung to the reality that Hadden and Ethan were apples and oranges.

Ethan, who had seemed so gruff and private, a solitary island of a man. Yet he actually wanted to spend time with her.

He was taking time out of his busy day to be with her.

Where Hadden, who loved to be in the public eye, had only been around when there was something in it for him—a chance to further his connections or feed his political ambitions. He'd never come around to take her to the fair or kissed her high atop the Ferris wheel.

When Ethan captured her mouth with his, thoughts of Hadden scattered. After several heated minutes when they finally came up for air, she realized their car was stopped at the very top.

The spring breeze was a little cool up there. It brought with it the faint sounds of the fair below. The people and the other rides on the midway looked magical and tiny from this vantage point. She felt a million miles away from everyone who could hurt her, everyone she could disappoint.

"You're quiet," Ethan said. "Everything okay?"

"I was just thinking I'm glad I'm not afraid of heights. It's nice up here."

"Yeah, I can't think of anyplace I'd rather be right now. I'm starting to remember what it's like to live again, to have feelings for someone again. Until now, it's like I've existed in a fog."

He kissed her again.

When the Ferris wheel jerked into motion, he leaned in so that his forehead was resting on hers. All she knew was she wished they could stay like this forever. Because up here in the clouds, only the best things seemed possible. This thing between them seemed real. It seemed like it could actually work.

## Chapter Eleven

Chelsea and Ethan stayed at the fair until early evening. After a quick check-in at Juliette's house to take care of Franklin, they'd grabbed a nice dinner at a steak house in downtown Celebration and spent the night at Juliette's because Chelsea felt guilty about leaving Franklin alone all day. He was sure to miss his mom since she wouldn't be home for another two days. But not *that* guilty. It had been a wonderful day. One of those gift days that was so unexpected and so perfect, it couldn't have gone better if she'd planned every detail. That was the thing, days like this weren't planned. They were lovely presents in beautiful wrapping—like a day at the fair and spending the night in Ethan's arms.

The next morning, Chelsea dressed in blue jeans

and a simple blue cotton blouse. She and Ethan had plans to go riding this afternoon, but first she needed to get some work done over at the barn. Lucy was meeting her there at nine o'clock and they needed to get a lot accomplished today to make sure everything was ready for the party. Chelsea planned to go in early to get a jump on things since Lucy had held down the fort yesterday while she was at the fair with Ethan, insisting that Chelsea take the day off.

After she applied a quick coat of mascara and dabbed on some lip gloss, Chelsea dried her hair in the hall bathroom. She couldn't stop thinking about how natural it was becoming to wake up next to Ethan every morning. Okay, so it had only happened twice, but that was the point. It felt as if they'd been together a lot longer. They were so comfortable together—not in a boring, too familiar way. It just felt right—seeing his face first thing when she opened her eyes; him in the kitchen making coffee for them; her getting ready for the day; them sitting down to breakfast together.

She turned off the blowdryer and set it down, staring at herself as realization engulfed her. This *thing* that was happening between them really could work.

More than that, she *wanted* it to work. She'd never met anyone who made her feel so safe, so whole, so adored. Yesterday he'd told her he had feelings for her, that everything had changed the moment he'd caught her coming in through that bathroom window.

She turned and looked at the window over the tub. It looked like any other unobtrusive bathroom window, yet the butterflies swarmed as she remembered that night. Who knew that an act of desperation—one that had nearly brought the police—would change her life?

Acknowledging the possibility for them made it suddenly hard to breathe. She braced her palms on the counter and inhaled sharply, half checking to see if the madness of this feeling would pass, but it clung to her like a second skin. This was night and day from how it had been with Hadden. She'd broken up with Hadden because she couldn't see a future with him. She could never love him like *this*. This is how it was supposed to be.

Here she was falling in love with Ethan Campbell. It was the last thing she'd wanted, the last thing she'd intended to do, when she left London to come to Celebration, but here she was with her heart in her hands, fully prepared to offer it to him.

What was more was she was pretty sure not only would he take it, but that he would handle it with the same mix of kid gloves and fierce protectiveness that he handled everything else that meant so much to him.

She went back into the bedroom, brushed her hair and pulled it back into a ponytail. She sat on the edge of the bed and tugged on her red Doc Marten's boots. They weren't exactly work boots—and they certainly weren't cowboy boots—but they were the best bet for the job. She remembered what he'd told her about his ex-wife, Molly, about how the breakup of his marriage had taught him that you could love someone but never really know that person. The bad experience had made him cautious and in the course of being careful he'd stopped living. He'd told her yesterday it was as if he had been existing in a fog, and then he'd opened up and confessed that since he'd met her, he was starting to remember what it was like to feel again, to live again.

She took her time lacing up the boots because she knew when she went into the kitchen, she had to tell Ethan the rest of her story. No more stalling. No more excuses.

If they could just get past this, the truth would set them free. But *being honest* was key.

She had to check herself for a moment to examine why she wasn't giving Ethan enough credit to see this as not a big deal. It was her own trust issues rearing their ugly heads. Even if she hadn't loved Hadden enough to see a future with him, she'd trusted him and he'd betrayed her. Now she was going to have to reopen that wound, and all the humiliation that went along with it, and confess that not only had she been pretending to be someone else from the moment she'd come in through that window, but that the reason she was running was because she'd embarrassed herself and her family.

But if Ethan was falling for her, if he was willing to trust her with his heart—to trust again for the first time since his marriage—she owed him the truth.

Her stomach knotted at the thought. But she couldn't put this off any longer. She checked her reflection in the full-length mirror one last time, squared her shoulders and started toward the kitchen, saying a silent prayer that he wouldn't walk out on her once he met the real Chelsea.

Ethan's kitchen repertoire wasn't vast. In fact, it was pretty lean. But he certainly wasn't starving. Bacon and fried eggs was his go-to breakfast. He grilled a mean steak; he could scare up a pot of chili that had garnered an honorable mention at the annual Celebration Chili Cook-off, and he was working on a top secret barbecue sauce recipe for the local pit master competition later this summer. But banana pancakes were his breakfast specialty—the secret weapon he pulled out when he was trying to make a good impression…or when he was falling in love. Actually, the only other woman he'd made them for was Molly, and she wasn't even a big fan of pancakes. But when he'd seen the ripe banana in Juliette's kitchen, he'd been inspired to make them for Chelsea.

He was just setting the plate with the pancakes in the oven to keep them warm until Chelsea finished getting ready when his phone rang.

The phone's display showed the name Ben Harper, his stable hand.

"Morning, Ben. Whatcha need?"

"Hey, Ethan, sorry to bother you so early, but Lulabelle has gone into labor. Tyler is with her now. Thought you'd want to know in case you wanted to come on out before your rounds."

Lulabelle was another one of the Triple C's highbred ventures. They bred her with a stallion that had fathered a Thoroughbred that had won the Triple

Crown a few years back. Ethan knew she was close to foaling. But did it have to be now?

He must be pretty far gone on Chelsea if he was grousing about this important business venture. He had to check his attitude. Chelsea could enjoy the banana pancakes without him. It just meant he'd have to make it up to her.

As if on cue, she entered the kitchen, clutching the coffee mug he'd brought her first thing and looking so damn good it set him back on his heels. There had been a time after he and Molly had divorced, when the pain was still fresh, that he thought he might never be able to feel this way again.

Sure, he needed time to heal, but maybe the reason it had taken so long was because he was waiting for Chelsea. Of course, he hadn't known it at the time—who could know something like that except in hindsight? But damn, this was good and she was worth the wait.

"Good morning, beautiful," he said.

"Good morning." Traces of her British accent were stronger than usual. She probably wasn't fully awake yet, but he liked the sexy rasp of her voice.

She walked over to the coffeepot and poured herself another cup. With her back still turned, she said, "Ethan, I'm sorry to do this so early, but we need to talk."

*We need to talk.*

The four words no man who was falling in love ever wanted to hear. Suddenly, he was glad to have a legitimate reason to put off this *talk*.

"Are you okay?" he asked.

She turned around and her face was so clouded with emotion that she didn't even have to answer. Whatever she was about to lay on him wasn't good. Hell, he should've known better than to get carried away.

"I hate to do this," he said. "But my stable hand just called and I have a horse in labor. I have to get out there now. Can we talk tonight?"

She nodded. Maybe he was imagining it, but he could've sworn she looked a little relieved. Maybe he was searching for any glimmer of hope. Maybe he was deluding himself.

"If this is moving too fast for you, we can slow it down to a comfortable pace." He grabbed a pot holder and took the plate with the pancakes out of the oven, removed the foil and set them on the table. "Eat breakfast and let's not rush to any rash conclusions. Let's talk about it later, okay?"

Chelsea tried. She really did. She'd gone out there and told him that they needed to talk but he had that emergency and just like that, fate had granted her a few more hours.

As she worked in the barn she tried to figure out if this was a blessing or a torment. Choosing to look at the positive, she racked her brain for something—anything that would allow her to make the most of the reprieve.

But how?

What could she do to turn this around?

She took out her frustrations sanding a rough board that might be a source of splinters if a guest leaned up against it.

Of course, it wasn't a given that Ethan would run. He might take it all in stride... He might even think it was sexy... Um, no. She wouldn't want a man who thought like that.

But he probably would take his cue from her delivery. If she presented it as if the hangman was coming, he would of course see it as gloom and doom.

Oh, bloody hell. If only it were that easy. Ethan had a mind of his own and it was highly unlikely that she would be able to lead him to the emotional conclusion she wanted him to have. He would think what he thought. She needed to prepare for the worst, but hope for the best.

The tape did not represent who she was and if he was scared off that easily, he wasn't the man for her. She had enough negativity in her life; she didn't need someone who couldn't stand by her when the chips were down.

Too bad her heart didn't see it that way.

"Hey, girl!" Lucy's bubbly voice filled the air. "You're here early."

Chelsea forced a smile. "I have a lot to do to make up for my absence yesterday."

Lucy waved her away. "Are you kidding? You deserved a break, as hard as you've been working. Did you have fun? You and my brother certainly have been spending a lot of time together. I haven't seen much of him, and when I have seen him he has been like a changed man. I don't know what you're doing to him, but keep on doing it. Um… That sounded vaguely dirty. So consider it rhetorical."

Chelsea couldn't help but laugh. While she had no desire to discuss Ethan's and her sex life with Lucy—or with anyone for that matter—Lucy might be able to help her with something else.

Chelsea set down the piece of sandpaper. "I've been meaning to say, I appreciate how you've kept my secret, Lucy."

Lucy's right eyebrow shot up. "Certain people may find me lacking in certain areas, but one thing no one can accuse me of is betraying a friend when I have given my word about something."

*A friend.*

Lucy really did consider her a friend and it touched Chelsea to the very core of her being. She had a lot of acquaintances, a lot of hangers-on—people who wanted something from her, or more aptly her brother, Thomas, who could do political favors, or her sister, who could serve as a stepping stone into the fashion industry. Chelsea, of course, could provide an introduction to both of them. She was a quick study. It only took being used a couple of times before the wall went up and the lock on the gate to her intimate circle stayed securely in place.

Lucy wanted nothing from her. Well, okay, Lucy wanted something from her. But at least she was up front about it. And Chelsea found that to be a breath of fresh air. This was a way she could contribute—a way that she could prove she was good at something.

Actually, Chelsea felt as if she was the one benefiting the most because she had finally found her place.

"You are a good friend, Lucy. I need to ask your opinion on something. I need your advice."

Lucy straightened her shoulders and leaned in toward her. "Of course. Is everything okay?"

Chelsea felt her eyes brimming and Lucy put her hand on Chelsea's arm. "Oh, my gosh. What's wrong? Let's go sit down."

They made their way over to the army trunk where Chelsea had sat with Ethan the day he'd brought her muffins. In many ways it was the day when everything had begun. Or at least one of the days. According to Ethan, everything had snapped into place for him the moment he saw her crawling in the window. Ha! What a sight that must've been.

"Okay, spill it," said Lucy. "What's wrong?"

"I have to tell your brother the truth."

Lucy's expression transformed from concern to puzzled to realization. She nodded. "I see. So I guess this means things between the two of you are pretty serious?"

Chelsea shrugged. "Maybe. Yes? I think so. Lucy, he told me he hasn't been this happy since things were good with Molly."

She stopped at that because it didn't feel right sharing any more intimacies. She had never been one to kiss and tell, and she knew how it felt to be betrayed by someone who did.

Lucy didn't push her any further. She simply nodded as if she understood perfectly. And she probably did.

"I started to tell him this morning, but he got called away on an emergency with one of the horses. I did say I needed to talk to him. We are getting together tonight." She knew she was rambling, but she needed to get it all out.

"He doesn't even know my real name. He doesn't know why I'm really here in Celebration. And most of all he doesn't know about the video."

She felt her face flame. "What's he going to think of me when he finds out?"

Lucy drew in a deep breath and looked as if she was weighing her words. "If this relationship is turning into something serious he needs to know the truth—"

Chelsea's phone chimed, signaling a text. Lucy's gaze fluttered down to Chelsea's phone. "Well, speak of the devil. That texter is my brother." A sly smile spread across her pretty face. "Go on, pick it up. I know you want to."

If it had been anyone else—or any other time in her life she would've ignored the text in favor of the conversation because it was just rude to let electronics dominate. But this was Ethan.

Bloody hell, she was in a bad way over him.

She purposely took her time picking up the phone and opening the text message so that she didn't appear as desperate as she felt.

What she saw nearly made her drop her phone. Ethan's text read:

Look at us. We made the paper. We're famous.

There was a picture of Ethan and her in a lip-lock in front of the kissing booth at the Celebration Spring Fair.

Apparently, the photo had gone out over the news-wire and the *Dallas Morning News* had run it on the front page of the entertainment section, promoting the fair as weekend fun.

If tabloid reporters were paying attention to the newswire or even if they had secured sources to be on the lookout, now they could track her to Celebration. The only thing she could do was leave before they got here and turned Ethan's life upside down.

## *Chapter Twelve*

The call came through minutes after she'd picked up Ethan's text. She'd barely had a chance to show Lucy the picture he'd sent when her phone rang. The sound startled her. At first she hoped against hope that it wasn't Ethan calling to get her reaction. But a minute later talking to Ethan seemed like a dream as she stared at the new message notification on her phone. She didn't recognize the number, but it was an international calling code and she knew who it was even before she picked up the message.

"Are you okay?" Lucy asked. "You look like you've seen a ghost."

"In a way I have. Actually, more of a monster than a ghost."

"Who is it?" Lucy demanded, taking Chelsea's

phone out of her hand and looking at the screen to see for herself. "Are you going to listen?"

Reflexively, Chelsea gave a quick shake of the head, as if Lucy had suggested she jump into a viper pit. Essentially, picking up the message, hearing that creepy voice, amounted to the same thing.

Still, there was a slim chance that she was wrong—maybe it was a family member calling from a different number; she hadn't talked to them since she'd landed Stateside. Now she'd given the press something else to write about. Even if she wasn't well-known in the States, a well-crafted story about a British noble hiding from scandal in the US might generate some interest. Especially if the creep used the angle that she was the sister of the likely new prime minister.

She could sit there and speculate all day. The only way she would know what she was dealing with was to listen to the message. She took a deep breath and pressed the playback icon and put it on speaker so Lucy could hear.

*"Lady Chelsea, you looked smashing in today's paper."* The cockney accent made her cringe. *"However, I am deeply troubled that if you were game to grant a photo that you didn't come to me. As you know, I do feel a bit proprietary when it comes to breaking news about you. Never fear, my darling, I'm getting a good sense of where you're hiding. Why don't you give your good pal Bertie a ring? You know I'll find you in a matter of days if you don't. Looking forward to seeing you. Toodles."*

"What the hell was that?" Lucy's eyes were so wide Chelsea was sure her friend would have nightmares.

"That monster is the reason I have to leave Celebration as soon as possible. This creep has been badgering me since university. I even changed my phone number before I left for the States, but he managed to get it. Now I'm afraid he will come here. I have no choice, Lucy. I have to leave."

"You always have a choice," Lucy said. "You don't have to run away from this son of a bitch. You need to tell Ethan and he will help you, Chelsea."

She shook her head again. "No. I can't. If I do, I'm afraid Ethan will go after him."

"Right," Lucy said. "That's the point."

"Wrong. The point is if Ethan goes after him—even if he enlists the help of the authorities—it will draw even more attention to the original story about the tape. I can't let that happen. I can't embarrass Ethan that way."

"Instead, you're going to break his heart?" Lucy said. "That's not much better, Chelsea."

"I've already made up my mind. I can't stay here and wait for Bertie Veal to find me and wreak havoc on the people who have so generously taken me in."

"You could get a restraining order," Lucy bargained. "Or what if you just sat down and reasoned with him? Isn't it worth a try, rather than running… again? You can't keep running, Chelsea."

She didn't want to keep running. She'd rather stay

right here with Ethan, maybe set up a design studio and make a life for herself—with him.

She thought about Lucy's suggestion of trying to bargain with him, but two seconds later she realized it was a bad idea.

"There is no bargaining with the devil, Lucy. You don't know who you're dealing with here. The guy is a parasite, a bully, a thug. He ticks just about every box that describes a sociopathic personality. He will stop at nothing to get a story that he can sell to the tabloids. He doesn't care if he destroys lives. That's how he makes his money. If he thinks you're trying to protect me, he will go after you. Think about what that could do to your new business, to Juliette's. He could ruin everything you've worked so hard for. Bertie Veal is the devil incarnate. My only choice is to leave before he tracks me to Celebration. I'm so sorry I can't stay for the grand opening party, but you're almost finished. You're almost there. You've got this. I know you're going to be a big success."

"I don't want you to go."

"I don't want to go, but I can't stay."

Lucy looked crestfallen and they sat and stared at each other for a moment that seemed like an impasse—two headstrong women who were used to getting what they wanted even when no one else could see the possibilities. Only this time what they wanted was beyond their reach—at least for now.

Finally, Lucy broke the silence. "Please promise you won't leave before you talk to Ethan."

Chelsea's stomach bunched and knotted. "Of course." She did owe him that much.

"How can you leave before the party?" Ethan said. "You promised Lucy you'd help her get to that point."

After Chelsea had left Lucy, she'd texted Ethan and asked him to come to Juliette's house after he'd finished with work. She had decided it was best to meet on neutral territory rather than asking him to meet her at his house or at the barn. While she waited for him, she booked herself on the first flight out of Dallas, packed and tidied up so that the place would be shipshape for Juliette. She'd called her friend to tell her about the turn of events and that Lucy had agreed to care for Franklin until Juliette returned. In similar fashion to Lucy, Juliette had tried to reason with her to stay—she suggested she tell Ethan and see if he could help get this guy off her back.

"You know, Chels, as long as you keep running, this guy will keep stalking you. You need to do something about it. If your folks won't help you, I can put you in touch with people who can."

"And it will get ugly before it gets better. I just can't put my family—and you and Ethan and Lucy— through any more crap."

"You know I love your family, but I'm disappointed in them for throwing you to the wolves."

"They might argue that I led the wolves to the door. Look, you know I love you. You're my best friend. Actually, you're family. I appreciate all that you've done—how you've let me disrupt your life hiding out here—but I have to handle this my way. It's time for me to go."

A knock sounded at the front door and Chelsea's heart leaped into her throat before it plummeted. "Ethan's here. I'm telling him everything. I need to go."

"Chels, call me later?"

"I will." With that, she disconnected the call and steeled herself to do the right thing.

Within the short span of five minutes, Chelsea saw Ethan's mood go from hopeful to flummoxed to prickly.

"I told Lucy from the start I might not be able to stay," Chelsea said when she tried to explain why she had to leave. "She knows it's time for me to go and she understands. I wish you would."

"I wish I understood, too. I thought things were good between us, Chelsea. Can you help me understand what went wrong? Can we at least talk about it?"

The look on his face was breaking her heart. He obviously thought she was rejecting him. She wasn't. If he only knew. She stared at her hands as if they might show her an answer. Or at least give her some direction about what to do next.

But of course, he didn't know the full story.

"Ethan, this morning when I said I needed to talk to you, it wasn't about me leaving. Actually, I didn't know I was leaving until later. Until after you sent me the photo from the paper."

"Now I really don't understand. What was so

reprehensible about that picture that it's driving you away?"

"There is nothing reprehensible about the picture. Ethan, I—"

She clamped her mouth shut. In the midst of this craziness, she'd almost told him she loved him. She did love him, but it didn't matter and it would only make things harder if she confessed her feelings.

So she did the only other thing possible. She told him the truth. "I haven't been completely honest with you, Ethan."

He was frowning at her, as if her revelation hadn't surprised him one bit. Had he known all along that she was hiding something? Of course he hadn't known. Still, he sat there, arms crossed, looking annoyed and defensive in his staunch silence.

The phrase *he who speaks first, loses* came to mind, but Chelsea knew there was no getting around it. She had to be the one to break the silence.

"Let me start from the beginning. The night I met you, I wasn't planning on running into anyone. I certainly wasn't planning on seeing you again or falling for you. My name isn't Chelsea Allen. It's Chelsea Ashford Alden. Chelsea Allen was a name that I used to use sometimes when Juliette and I would go out and I was trying to fly under the radar."

His brows drew together. "Fly under the radar? What does that mean? I understand that sometimes women don't want to be bothered, is that what you mean?"

"No, I mean fly under the radar, as in not being recognized."

"Why? Are you someone famous who I'm not familiar with?"

She shrugged. "Sort of. My father is the fifth Earl of Downing. My brother is Thomas Ashford Alden. Does that ring a bell?"

He did not look impressed, which was fine. She didn't expect him to be up on British politics.

"It's quite likely that my brother will be the next prime minister of Great Britain—"

"And you couldn't trust me with that?" He shook his head and got up and paced the length of the room. She wanted to give him time to let this sink in before she told him the real reason she was running.

"If your father is an earl, does that make you royalty or something?"

"Yes. Sort of. I'm at the very end of the line for the throne, but that doesn't mean anything."

"Well, yeah, it really does. It's who you are. Why didn't you tell me? I get using the fake name when we first met, but Chelsea, we've seen *a lot* more of each other since then. You could've told me. You could've trusted me."

The bottom dropped out of her stomach. This was it. This was the moment she'd been dreading. But she had to tell him. There was no holding back.

"Ethan, please sit down. There's more. There's a reason I lied to you."

She told him everything—about Bertie Veal, about the secret recording, about Hadden selling it to the tabloids after she broke up with him, about her parents' mandate, about running from the reporter who seemed hell-bent on ruining her life.

"He's bound to find me and I have to leave before he tracks me here—to you and Lucy and Juliette. You don't need that in your life. You don't need to be linked romantically to someone who is known around town as *that woman—the one in that video—wink, wink, nudge, nudge.*"

She paused and it was the stupidest thing—her heart thudded against her breastbone and she was hoping he would gather her in his arms and tell her everything would be all right, that he would love her and protect her and make sure that Bertie Veal never hurt her again. But he just sat there looking through her with a vaguely horrified expression on his face.

It was the look she'd feared since the moment she realized that she could love this man. But he had fallen for Chelsea Allen, a woman who didn't even exist.

Chelsea had been gone four days and Ethan had felt every ticking second like a dagger to the heart. Leave it to him to fall in love with a woman he couldn't have. That was why he hadn't gone after her, hadn't begged her to stay. This had nothing to do with inferiority complexes or male pride; he simply knew when he was facing an impossible battle. It wasn't that he was being a defeatist, he was being a realist.

It was clear from the moment Chelsea told him she was leaving that she couldn't wait to get out of this town. If Molly, who had been born and raised here, had been loath to stay, why would someone like Lady Chelsea Ashford Alden—someone of noble birth, who had gone to the same college as the Duke of Cambridge, the guy who would likely sit on the throne of England. Hell, the fact that Chelsea could even say she was in line for the throne was daunting. He refused to kid himself that someone like that would want to give up the jet set for life on a horse ranch that was rooted just as deeply in him as London was in her.

He wasn't even angry that she'd lied about her name and had evaded the truth about her background. Okay, he was at first, but not now. The reason he was letting her go without a fight was because it was simply good horse sense.

He was still a little too raw to contemplate the prospect of being *just friends.* After she'd told him about the video that creep had sold to the tabloids, Ethan had given in to curiosity and spent the better part of an afternoon online, searching the web for stories about Lady Chelsea Ashford Alden. He could not find the infamous video and he wouldn't have watched it if he had. He could only hope that somehow her well-connected family had been successful in helping her wipe the video off the internet.

One thing he did find online was a story about Chelsea and him that was written by Chelsea's stalker, titled, *Could This Be Love for Lady Chelsea or Just Another Spring Fling?* The con artist had ripped off the photo of Ethan kissing Chelsea at the fair, the one that had originally appeared in the *Dallas Morning News*.

Pain and a sense of loss as raw and real as the day that Chelsea had told him she was leaving stung every nerve ending in him, tempting him to sign off and leave well enough alone. But he couldn't. He wasn't sure if he was punishing himself or soothing himself by reading story after story about this woman he thought he knew.

Though the web seemed to be cleansed of the video, plenty of sensational and obviously fabricated stories remained. He came away from the search with the sound conclusion that the Chelsea Ashford Alden he saw on the web, the one depicted in all those trumped-up tabloid stories was not the same woman he'd fallen in love with. That was not Chelsea. The person in the tabloids was an exaggerated figment of a desperate reporter's imagination.

Chelsea wasn't any different than any other woman who had done her share of having a good time, raising a little innocent hell. At least she'd steered clear of substance abuse and she didn't let alcohol rule her days and nights. He'd witnessed that firsthand. No, the Chelsea Ashford Alden he'd met was kind and generous and decent. She was also beautiful and charismatic and the daughter of a well-connected, high-profile family. That made her the perfect target for a sleazebag like Bertie Veal.

It also didn't change the fact that she was in England and he was in Texas. Lady Chelsea Ashford Alden would never be content in a small town like

Celebration. So Ethan threw himself into his work at the Triple C and pretended that he didn't have a huge gaping hole in his chest where his heart used to live.

## Chapter Thirteen

On the day of the grand opening party, which was a trial run before hosting Connor Bryce's wedding reception, Ethan dressed in khaki slacks and a plaid button-down that he had taken the time to press so that he'd look presentable for Lucy's big night.

He had to give credit where credit was due. She had stuck to her guns and brought this dream to fruition. He was proud of his little sister. That was why he was determined to make this night about her, not about the person who was conspicuously absent tonight. He missed Chelsea. The ache lingered like arthritis in his soul. But as with all adversity he'd ever faced in his life, he learned to live with the pain, to push through it and carry on.

Tonight would be no different. He would go to the

party, help Lucy however he could—though Juliette, party planner extraordinaire, seemed to have everything under control. He would be there as a source of support and do his best not to think of Chelsea.

She'd been gone two weeks now. Every single day of that time he'd had to consciously restrain himself from calling her. His heart longed to see her one more time, but his head reminded him it was hopeless. He wasn't looking for a long-distance relationship. He certainly wasn't about to pin his hopes on her having a big change of heart and trading in the glitz and glam of London for him at the Triple C Ranch.

That was just how it was. The truth hurt, but as with everything else he would survive. Or so he told himself. It had become his mantra. If he repeated it enough, someday he might believe it.

The party started at seven. He wasn't much for shindigs like this. So when he'd called Lucy and asked her if she wanted him to come early and she had assured him she and Juliette had everything under control, he decided to do his evening rounds of the ranch, checking to make sure everything was buttoned up for the night.

The sun was hanging low in the western sky, bathing everything in soft tones of gold and orange, red and blue, showing off as it bid the world good-night and prepared to tuck itself away. Another day done. Since she had been gone he'd started feeling a little sadder at this time of night. During the day, when the sun was hotter than the hinges of hell, it burned right through him, numbing the pain. The vast blackness of the night threw a cloak over his emotions. Thank God he hadn't reached for the bottle. He'd been tempted because it was the one sure way to anesthetize the pain. In fact, a couple of times he'd had to call his sponsor and have him talk the bottle out of his hand. He wasn't going to let losing her break him.

The urge for a drink was always the worst at twilight. He remembered his mom calling this time of night the *blue hour* and now he understood why.

Tonight, as with every night for the past two weeks, as he drove by the pastures and the stables he saw reminders of Chelsea everywhere he looked. In the shadows of the oak trees, in the distance by the post and rail fence, in the rolling hills that graced his land. Her specter lived there.

How long was it going to take to exorcise her?

This morose thought was particularly irritating because she wasn't dead. He couldn't even pretend like she was dead to him. He couldn't hate her. He couldn't call her names or scoff at her way of life because he still loved her. The only thing she was guilty of was coming from a different world—and for that matter, he was just as damn guilty as she was. Actually, he shouldered more of the guilt for not trying to meet her halfway. For letting her go without trying to salvage something of them or letting her know he was willing to be her friend. They could do that long distance, couldn't they? Couldn't they be friends?

No. He didn't want to be her friend.

But for the first time since she'd left, he realized that he wasn't good with completely cutting her out of his life. He had no idea how she felt because they hadn't talked. No one had made the first move to reach out to the other. Suddenly, it seemed ludicrous not to man up.

Glancing at the dashboard clock that glowed neon-green, he noted the hour and his brain calculated the time difference between Celebration and London: six hours. If it was seven thirty here, that meant it was one thirty in the morning there. It was late. But it was a Saturday night. He wondered what she was doing. Was she home asleep? Or was she out with friends… or out on a date? Even though he had no right, the thought kicked him in the gut.

He pulled the truck over and took out his phone. He brought up the last text they had exchanged, the one where she had asked him to meet her at Juliette's house the night everything went down. For about the millionth time, he racked his brain, trying to think of something he could've done differently that might've changed the way things turned out.

Of course he came up with nothing. Except the nagging reminder that he could've asked her to stay. But he couldn't ask her to trade in the big city for small-town life. And he was back at square one.

This train of thought had become part of his nightly routine and was as intrinsic to him as doing rounds of the property.

What a terrible way to end things. He'd been so caught off guard by her revelation. He'd honestly thought she had called him there to say she needed space, that things were moving too fast for her. He'd been idiot enough to believe all he had to do to make things right was give her a little room and she would realize how right they were together. Hell, he didn't need to be joined at the hip with the woman he loved, but he sure as hell needed the two of them to want the same things. Been there done that with someone who wasn't on the same page. It never ended well.

The reality check still wasn't resonating. It was bouncing around his brain like a ping-pong ball, but the message of good sense wasn't reaching his heart.

He scrolled up past the text that had decided their fate and read happier messages.

Chelsea: What do you want to do for dinner tonight?

Ethan: I'd like to have you in my bed.

Ethan: Want to go riding this afternoon?

Chelsea: Are you talking horses or...? :)

The playfulness made him smile through the ache. If someone didn't know better they might think the relationship was solely based on sex—and God, the sex had been off the charts. It had rocked his world. But there had been so much more.

If he texted her now, she'd get his message first thing in the morning... That banked on her being home sleeping. If he texted her, she could reply whenever she was ready.

He scrolled past the record of them, back to the blank screen and typed:

Hi, doing my rounds of the ranch. Realized that we never got to go riding. The next time you visit Jules, let's make that happen.

He started to delete the message. In fact, he did erase the part that said *let's make that happen*, but after staring at it for a while, trying to figure out what to write instead, something that didn't sound bitter or pathetic or too presumptuous— For God's sake was he actually sitting here second-guessing himself over a text message?

It was a text to a friend. Nothing more. So he re-typed it and pushed Send before he could talk himself out of it. The overwhelming urge to wash away the sickening insecurity with a tall, cold draft nearly overwhelmed him. He gripped the steering wheel with both hands until the wave passed.

He was better than that. He'd worked too damn hard to get where he was, to stay sober this long and rebuild his life, to fall off the wagon tonight. He needed to go put in an appearance at Lucy's party and then he would get the hell out of there.

As he reached for the gear shift, his phone signaled an incoming text.

His gut tightened as he picked up the phone and saw Chelsea's response.

Hello, stranger. Good to hear from you. You must be a mind reader. I was thinking about you and Lucy.

Tonight is the big grand opening trial run, isn't it? How is it going?

I'm on my way to the party now. I know it's late there. I hope the text didn't wake you.

You didn't wake me. I'm at a party myself. My love to you and Lucy. I'm there in spirit.

Since she was out on the town, he debated whether or not to respond—it didn't escape him that she hadn't picked up on the bit about going riding. But both of them knew that was just an icebreaker. He wasn't going to hold his breath, waiting for her to come back to Celebration. Maybe if they corresponded as friends, someday he would make the trip to visit her in London. It was already feeling complicated. That was why he decided a quick *gotta go* reply would be the best way to keep it casual.

Thx. I'll share your message with Lucy when I get there. Talk to you soon.

He tossed his phone onto the passenger seat and drove to the barn. The parking lot was already crowded with cars and trucks. It looked like the entire town of Celebration had turned out to support Lucy's new endeavor.

He managed to maneuver his truck into a space on the unpaved area behind the building and made a mental note to mention to Lucy that she should consider adding more paved parking. As he rounded the barn heading toward the front door, he could hear the sound of a band playing a Luke Bryan tune mixed with the convivial sound of happy people at a party. Good for Lucy. He hadn't realized it before, but this really was her wheelhouse. If anyone knew how to have fun, it was his sister. And he truly meant that in the most supportive way. He checked himself before he opened the door, which was festooned with twinkling white lights and a wreath made of wheat stalks and checked ribbon.

Just because he wasn't in the mood for a party didn't mean he would bring the shade to his sister's big night. As his hand rested on the door handle, he wondered if he should've brought her flowers to celebrate the occasion. He even considered leaving to get some, but he knew it was as much a stall tactic as it was a congratulatory gesture for her. The best gift he could give her was his presence and a good attitude.

And the sooner he did this, the sooner he could leave.

He pulled open the door and stepped inside and through the throngs of people, the first person he saw was Chelsea.

When Chelsea caught sight of Ethan, her knees almost buckled. She had been nervous about making the trip, but she had wanted to be there for Lucy. The two of them had kept in touch since she'd left Celebration. She'd been giving Lucy final design advice. The Campbell Wedding Barn still had a long way to go before the place would be finished, but it was present-able enough to serve as a rustic venue. They'd work out the kinks in this trial run grand opening party so that they'd be as prepared as possible to give Connor Bryce and his bride the wedding reception of their dreams. But that was Juliette's and Lucy's territory. She would make sure the place looked as fabulous as possible.

Lucy had all but begged her to come back for the party. The tipping point happened when she'd learned that her brother's old university pal, who was now a high-powered barrister, was able to help cleanse the internet of the offending video and teach Bertie Veal and Hadden Hastings a lesson. Not only did Thomas's mate scare the bejabbers out of both men by threaten-ing an invasion of privacy lawsuit—referencing the civil suit against Gawker Media was enough to keep Hadden in check—but Thomas's chum had also im-plied that if Mr. Veal persisted in stalking Chelsea, he just might find it difficult to gain reentry to the United Kingdom if he left again. It seemed old Ber-tie had some past indiscretions that had as of yet re-mained unflagged, but that could easily be changed with a couple of phone calls.

Thomas's friend assured Bertie and Hadden they were welcome to challenge him, but they would cer-tainly end up wishing they'd left well enough alone. It was their choice: mess with Chelsea and suffer conse-quences, or refrain from harassing the Ashford Alden family and have a happy life. The choice was en-tirely theirs.

The gauntlet was leveled a couple of weeks ago, and neither Bertie nor Hadden had so much as glanced in Chelsea's direction.

It was almost like starting over. She'd realized that the place she wanted to make her fresh start was Celebration, Texas.

Of course, she had no guarantee that Ethan would welcome her with open arms. The text he'd sent had been the first communication they'd exchanged since the horrible night when everything crashed and burned.

Just because his text had been warm, it didn't mean he wanted anything beyond friendship—not after her confession that she had lied to him.

As she watched him walk toward her, the butterflies that he always seemed to induce had come to life again, proving that she still had it bad for him. No, not just bad—oh, who was she kidding? She was in love with the guy and in this moment, she wanted nothing more than to win him back. She had no idea how he felt about her, but she was going to exhaust every avenue before she gave up on Ethan Campbell.

As he closed the distance between them, she was so giddy-nervous she thought she might jump out of her skin. She clutched her cranberry and soda so tightly she had to make a conscious effort to loosen her grip so that the glass didn't burst in her hand. She raised the other hand in a shy greeting as he approached.

She couldn't read his expression. His eyes were intense but his face was otherwise neutral. She couldn't figure out if it was a shocked-but-happy-to-see-her neutral or if he was coming over to ask her to leave.

She found her words in the nick of time. "Great party, huh?"

"You're here. You came back."

"I wouldn't have missed this for the world."

He opened his mouth to say something but shut it again, his brow furrowing as if he was trying to process everything. Finally, he said, "It seemed so final when you left."

She swallowed the lump in her throat. "That was before I knew that Celebration was a safe place—*my* safe place."

The side of his mouth quirked up into that half smile that she missed as much as a drowning woman missed air. She hadn't realized how much she missed it—how desperately she'd missed him—until now. She'd been pining for him, but the magnitude of it hadn't hit until this very moment.

The pull of attraction was strong, but attraction alone wasn't what Chelsea needed. She needed to know that Ethan could forgive her. That maybe, just maybe, he could love her for who she was, despite her stupid mistakes and everything that made her who she was. Because she loved him.

"You never answered my question about going riding."

"I figured we have plenty of time for that since I'm moving back."

She hoped he'd meant it. That it wasn't just a rhetorical conversation starter.

"Did you really mean it, Ethan?" Crap. She hadn't meant to say that out loud. But she did and there was no taking it back now. "Because I hope you did. I mean, I hope you meant you want to go riding with me. Because after I left I was afraid that you never wanted to speak to me again, much less see me again. I never meant to lie to you. I don't make a habit of lying to people I care about. But I realize you might feel like you don't even know me. I wouldn't blame you if you never wanted to see me again."

"You're wrong about that—on both accounts. I know who you are now and I understand why you did what you thought you had to do. I couldn't care less about the video. I didn't watch it."

"It's gone now," she said. "Thomas worked his magic and took care of it and Bertie Veal. He won't be bothering me—us—anymore. That's the thing about big brothers—"

"I love you, Chelsea. Why would I never want to see you again?"

His words—those three words—made the room expand and contract and then tilt on its axis. When she finally regained her equilibrium, she said, "Well, that's good to know because I love you, too, and I was really hoping that we could talk about what we were going to do about this love predicament we seem to have found ourselves in. If we're in love, it seems a little counterproductive to not talk and not see each other. In fact, I'll confess that I don't think I've ever been as miserable as I've been these last weeks that

I was in London. I had so many things I wanted to talk to you about and—"

The next thing she knew her world actually was tipping on its axis because Ethan had gathered her in his arms and had smothered her rambling words as he covered her mouth with his.

"That's what we're going to do about it," he said after he righted her and set her back on her feet.

Her head was spinning, but she had enough presence of mind to say, "So, you don't think it's a bad idea for me to move to Celebration and open a design business?"

Ethan pulled her close and whispered in her ear. "That's the best idea I've heard in ages. The only thing that would make me happier is if you'll marry me. I nearly let you get away once, but I won't let that happen again."

Her entire body zinged with elation. "Ethan Campbell, are you proposing to me?"

"I don't have a ring, because I hadn't exactly planned this." He fell to one knee. "Chelsea Ashford Alden, will you make me the happiest man alive and agree to be my wife?"

Before she could answer, she realized the music had stopped playing and every eye in the house was watching them.

"Yes!"

The room erupted into a rousing round of applause and the band began the strains of a romantic country love song that Chelsea recognized but couldn't recall the name of.

"This is for the happy couple," the singer said and everyone cleared a path so that Chelsea and Ethan could have the dance floor.

As they swayed to the song, she gazed into his eyes. "Let the records show that not only was that the most romantic proposal ever," she said, "but probably one of the most spontaneous, too. No one will ever call you unspontaneous again."

"I don't care what anybody calls me as long as they call me your husband."

\* \* \* \* \*

*Don't miss Lucy Campbell's story, up next in the*
CELEBRATION, TX *miniseries,*
*coming in July 2017!*

*But first, look for Nancy Robards Thompson's contribution to* THE FORTUNES OF TEXAS: THE SECRET FORTUNES *continuity, available May 2017, only from Harlequin Special Edition.*

*Can't get enough romance? Keep reading for a special preview of WILD HORSE SPRINGS, the latest engrossing novel in the* RANSOM CANYON *series by* New York Times *bestselling author Jodi Thomas, coming in February 2017 from HQN Books!*

CODY WINSLOW THUNDERED through the night on a half-wild horse that loved to run. The moon followed them, dancing along the edge of the canyon as they darted over winter buffalo grass that was stiff with frost.

The former Texas Ranger watched the dark outline of the earth where the land cracked open wide enough for a river to run at its base.

The canyon's edge seemed to snake closer, as if it were moving, crawling over the flat plains, daring Cody to challenge death. One missed step might take him and the horse over the rim and into the black hole. They'd tumble maybe a hundred feet down, barreling over jagged rocks and frozen juniper branches as sharp as spears. No horse or man would survive.

Only, tonight Cody wasn't worried. He needed to ride, to run, to feel adrenaline pumping in his veins, to know he was alive. He rode hoping to outrun his dark mood. The demons that were always in his mind were chasing him tonight. Daring him. Betting him to take one more risk…the one that would finally kill him.

"Run," he shouted to the midnight mare. Nothing would catch him here. Not on his land. Not over land his ancestors had hunted on for thousands of years. Fought over. Died for and bled into. Apache blood, settler blood, Comanchero blood mixed in him as it did in this part of Texas. His family tree was a tumbleweed of every kind of tribe that ever crossed the plains.

If the horse fell and they went to their deaths, no one would find them for weeks on this far corner of his ranch. Even the canyon that snaked off the great Palo Duro had no name here. It wasn't beautiful like Ransom Canyon, with layers of earth revealed in a rainbow of colors. Here the rocks were jagged, shooting out of the deep earthen walls from twenty feet in some places, almost like a thin shelf.

The petrified-wood formations along the floor of the canyon reminded Cody of snipers waiting, unseen but deadly. Cody felt numb, already dead inside, as he raced across a place with no name on a horse he called Midnight.

The horse's hooves tapped suddenly over a low place where water ran off the flat land and into the canyon. Frozen now. Silent. Deadly black ice. For a moment the tapping matched Cody's heartbeat, then both horse and rider seemed to realize the danger at once.

Cody leaned back, pulling the reins, hoping to stop the animal in time, but the horse reared in panic. Dancing on her hind legs for a moment before twisting violently and bucking Cody off.

As Cody flew through the night air, he almost smiled. The battle he'd been fighting since he was shot and left for dead on the border three years ago was about to end here on his own land. The voices of all the ancestors who came before him whispered in the wind, as if calling him.

When he hit the frozen ground so hard it knocked the air from his lungs, he knew death wouldn't come easy tonight. Though he'd welcome the silence, Cody knew he'd fight to the end. He came from generations of fighters. He was the last of his line, and here in the dark he'd make his stand. Too far away to call for help. And too stubborn to ask, anyway.

As he fought to breathe, his body slid over a tiny river of frozen rain and into the black canyon.

He twisted, struggling to stop, but all he managed to do was tumble down. Branches whipped against him, and rocks punched his ribs with the force of a prizefighter's blow. And still he rolled. Over and over. Ice on his skin, warm blood dripping into his eyes. He tried bracing for the hits that came when he landed for a moment before his body rolled again. He grabbed for a rock or a branch to hold on to, but his leather gloves couldn't get a grip on the ice.

He wasn't sure if he managed to relax or pass out, but when he landed on a flat rock near the bottom of the canyon, total blackness surrounded him and the few stars above offered no light. For a while he lay still, aware that he was breathing. A good sign. He hurt all over. More proof he was alive.

He'd been near death before. He knew that sometimes the body turned off the pain. Slowly, he mentally took inventory. There were parts that hurt like hell. Others he couldn't feel at all.

Cody swore as loud as he could and smiled. At least he had his voice. Not that anyone would hear him in the canyon. Maybe his brain was mush; he obviously had a head wound. The blood kept dripping into his eyes. His left leg throbbed with each heartbeat and he couldn't draw a deep breath. He swore again.

He tried to move and pain skyrocketed, forcing him to concentrate to stop shaking. Fire shot up his leg and flowed straight to his heart. Cody took shallow breaths and tried to reason. He had to control his breathing. He had to stay awake or he'd freeze. He had to keep fighting. Survival was bone and blood to his nature.

The memory of his night in the mud near the Rio Grande came back as if it had been only a day ago, not three years. He'd been bleeding then, hurt, alone. Four rangers had stood on the bank at dusk. He'd seen the other three crumple when bullets fell like rain.

Only, it had been hot that night, so silent after all the gunfire. Cody had known that every ranger in the area would be looking for him at first light; he had to make it to dawn first. Stay alive. They'd find him.

But not this time.

No one would look for him tonight or tomorrow. No one would even notice he was gone. He'd made sure of that. He'd left all his friends back in Austin after the shooting. He'd broken up with his girlfriend, who'd said she couldn't deal with hospitals. When he came back to his family's land, he didn't bother to call any of his old friends. He'd grown accustomed to the solitude. He'd needed it to heal not just the wounds outside, but the ones deep inside.

Cody swore again.

The pain won out for a moment and his mind drifted. At the corners of his consciousness, he knew he needed to move, stop the bleeding, try not to freeze, but he'd become an expert at drifting that night on the border. Even when a rifle had poked into his chest as one of the drug runners tested to see if he was alive, Cody hadn't reacted.

If he had, another bullet would have gone into his body, which was already riddled with lead.

Cody recited the words he'd once had to scrub off the walls in grade school. Mrs. Presley had kept repeating as he worked, *Cody Winslow, you'll die cussing if you don't learn better.*

Turned out she might be right. Even with his eyes almost closed, the stars grew brighter and circled around him like drunken fireflies. If this was death's door, he planned to go through yelling.

The stars drew closer. Their light bounced off the black canyon walls as if they were sparks of echoes.

He stopped swearing as the lights began to talk.

"He's dead," one high, bossy voice said. "Look how shiny the blood is."

Tiny beams of light found his face, blinding him to all else.

A squeaky sound added, "I'm going to throw up. I can't look at blood."

"No, he's not dead," another argued. "His hand is twitching and if you throw up, Marjorie Martin, I'll tell Miss Adams."

All at once the lights were bouncing around him, high voices talking over each other.

"Yes, he is dead."

"Stop saying that."

"You stop saying anything."

"I'm going to throw up."

Cody opened his eyes. The lights were circling around him like a war party.

"See, I told you so."

One beam of light came closer, blinding him for a moment, and he blinked.

"He's hurt. I can see blood bubbling out of him in several spots." The bossy voice added, "Don't touch it, Marjorie. People bleeding have germs."

The gang of lights streamed along his body as if trying to torture him or drive him mad as the world kept changing from black to bright. It occurred to him that maybe he was being abducted by aliens, but he doubted the beings coming to conquer the world would land here in West Texas or that they'd sound like little girls.

"Hell," he said and to his surprise the shadows all jumped back.

After a few seconds he made out the outline of what might be a little girl, or maybe ET.

"You shouldn't cuss, mister. We heard you way

back in the canyon yelling out words I've seen written but never knew how to pronounce."

"Glad I could help with your education, kid. Any chance you have a cell phone or a leader?"

"We're not allowed to carry cell phones. It interferes with our communicating with nature." She shone her flashlight in his eyes. "Don't call me *kid*. Miss Adams says you should address people by their names. It's more polite. My name is Melanie Miller and I could read before I started kindergarten."

Cody mumbled a few words, deciding he was in hell already and, who knew, all the helpers' names started with *M*.

All at once the lights went jittery again and every one of the six little girls seemed to be talking at the same time.

One thought he was too bloody to live. One suggested they should cover him with their coats; another voted for undressing him. Two said they would never touch blood. One wanted to put a tourniquet around his neck.

Cody was starting to hope death might come faster when another shadow carrying a lantern moved into the mix. "Move back, girls. This man is hurt."

He couldn't see more than an outline, but the new arrival was definitely not a little girl. Tall, nicely shaped, hiking boots, a backpack on her back.

Closing his eyes and ignoring the little girls' constant questions, he listened as a calm voice used her cell to call for help. She had the location down to latitude and longitude and described a van parked in an open field about a hundred yards from her location where they could land a helicopter. When she hung up, she knelt at his side and shifted the backpack off her shoulder.

As she began to check his injuries, her voice calmly gave instructions. "Go back to the van, girls. Two at a time, take turns flashing your lights at the sky toward the North Star. The rest of you get under the blankets and stay warm. When you hear the chopper arrive, you can watch from the windows, but stay in the van.

"McKenna, you're in charge. I'll be back as soon as they come."

Another *M*, Cody thought, but didn't bother to ask.

To his surprise the gang of ponytails marched off like tiny little soldiers.

"How'd you find me?" Cody asked the first of a dozen questions bouncing around in his aching head as the woman laid out supplies from her pack.

"Your cussing echoed off the canyon wall for twenty miles." Her hands moved along his body, not in a caress, but to a man who hadn't felt a woman's touch in years, it wasn't far from it.

"Want to give me your name? Know what day it is? What year? Where you are?"

"I don't have brain damage," he snapped, then regretted moving his head. "My name's Winslow. I don't care what day it is or what year for that matter." He couldn't make out her face. "I'm on my own land. Or at least I was when my horse threw me."

She might have been pretty if she wasn't glaring

at him. The lantern light offered that flashlight-to-the-chin kind of glow.

"Where does it hurt?" She kept her voice low, but she didn't sound friendly. "As soon as I pass you to the medics, I'll start looking for your horse. The animal might be out here, too, hurting or dead. Did he fall with you?"

Great! His Good Samaritan was worried more about the horse than him. "I don't know. I don't think so. When I fell off the edge of the canyon, Midnight was still standing, probably laughing at me." He took a breath as the woman moved to his legs. "I tumbled for what seemed like miles. It hurts all over."

"How did this happen?"

"The horse got spooked when we hit a patch of ice," he snapped again, tired of talking, needing all his strength to handle the pain. Cusswords flowed out with each breath. Not at her, but at his bad luck.

She ignored them as she brushed over the left leg of his jeans already stained dark with blood. He tried to keep from screaming. He fought her hand as she searched, examining, and he knew he couldn't take much more without passing out.

"Easy," she whispered as her blood-warmed fingers cupped his face. "Easy, cowboy. You've got a bad break. I have to do what I can to stabilize you and slow the blood flow. They'll be here soon. You've got to let me wrap a few of these wounds so you don't bleed out."

He nodded once, knowing she was right.

In the glow of a lantern she worked, making a

tourniquet out of his belt, carefully wrapping his leg, then his head wound.

Her voice finally came low, sexy maybe if it were a different time, a different place. "It looks bad, but I don't see any chunks of brain poking out anywhere."

He didn't know if she was trying to be funny or just stating a fact. He didn't bother to laugh. She put a bandage on the gash along his throat. It wasn't deep, but it dripped a steady stream of blood.

As she wrapped the bandage, her breasts brushed against his cheek, distracting him. If this was her idea of doctoring a patient with no painkillers, it was working. For a few seconds there, he almost forgot to hurt.

"I don't have water to clean the wounds, but the dressing should keep anything else from getting in."

Cody began to calm. The pain was still there, but the demons in the corners of his mind were silent. Watching her move in the shadows relaxed him.

"Cody," he finally said. "My first name is Cody."

She smiled then for just a second.

"You a nurse?" he asked.

"No. I'm a park ranger. If you've no objection, I'd like to examine your chest next."

Cody didn't move as she unzipped his jacket. "I used to be a ranger, but I never stepped foot in a park." He could feel her unbuttoning his shirt. Her hand moved in, gently gliding across his ribs.

When he gasped for air, she hesitated, then whispered, "One broken rib." A moment later she added, "Two."

He forced slow, long breaths as he felt the cold night air pressing against his bare chest. Her hand crossed over his bruised skin, stopping at the scars he'd collected that night at the Rio Grande.

She lifted the light. "Bullet wounds?" she questioned more to herself than him. "You've been hurt bad before."

"Yeah," he said as he took back control of his mind and made light of a gunfight that almost ended his life. "I was fighting outlaws along the Rio Grande. I swear it seemed like that night almost two hundred years ago. Back when Captain Hays ordered his men to cross the river with guns blazing. We went across just like that, only chasing drug runners and not cattle rustlers like they did back then. But we were breaking the law not to cross just the same."

He closed his eyes and saw his three friends. They'd gone through training together and were as close as brothers. They wanted to fight for right. They thought they were invincible that night on the border, just like Captain Hays's men must have believed.

Only, those rangers had won the battle. They'd all returned to Texas. Cody had carried his best friend back across the water that night three years ago, but Hobbs hadn't made it. He'd died in the mud a few feet from Cody. Fletcher took two bullets but helped Gomez back across. Both men died.

"I've heard of that story about the famous Captain Hays." She brought him back from a battle that had haunted him every night for three years. "Legend is that not one ranger died that night. They rode across the Rio screaming and firing. The bandits thought there were a hundred of them coming. But, cowboy, if you rode with Hays, that'd make you a ghost tonight and you feel like flesh and blood to me. Today's rangers are not allowed to cross."

Her hand was moving over his chest lightly, caressing now, calming him, letting him know that she was near. He relaxed and wished they were somewhere warm.

"You're going to make it, Winslow. I have a feeling you're too tough to die easy."

*Don't miss WILD HORSE SPRINGS by*
New York Times *bestselling author Jodi Thomas,*
*available February 2017 wherever*
*HQN books and ebooks are sold!*
*www.Harlequin.com*

Copyright © 2017 by Jodi Koumalats

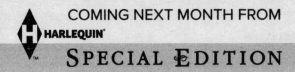

# COMING NEXT MONTH FROM

## HARLEQUIN®

# SPECIAL EDITION

## Available January 17, 2017

### #2527 HER SWEETEST FORTUNE
*The Fortunes of Texas: The Secret Fortunes* • by Stella Bagwell
Sophie Fortune Robinson is certain the office heartthrob is her one true love, but
when he turns out to be a dud, her friend Mason Montgomery is there to cheer
her up. As they spend more time together, will they be able to set aside their
insecurities to build a future together?

### #2528 HIS PREGNANT COURTHOUSE BRIDE
*Conard County: The Next Generation* • by Rachel Lee
An unexpected pregnancy has high-class lawyer Amber Towers heading for
Conard County—and Judge Wyatt Carter. Neither of them expected their
law-school attraction to still be this strong, but their fledgling feelings have to
weather Amber's wariness when it comes to love, not to mention nasty rumors
and an election season, if they want to make it to a courthouse wedding.

### #2529 BABY TALK & WEDDING BELLS
*Those Engaging Garretts!* • by Brenda Harlen
Widowed single dad Braden Garrett is looking for a mother for his adopted
daughter, Saige, and librarian Cassie MacKinnon is the perfect candidate! But
Cassie wants more than just a family—she wants a fairy-tale love to go along with
it, and Brad's not sure he'll ever be the man able to give it to her.

### #2530 THE COOK'S SECRET INGREDIENT
*Hurley's Homestyle Kitchen* • by Meg Maxwell
PI and single dad Carson Ford knows the fortune-teller who promised his dad
a second great love was a fraud. He just needs the fortune-teller's daughter,
Olivia Hurley, to explain that to his father. But the mystery woman sounds very
much like her estranged aunt, so they set out to find her and just might find love
for themselves along the way.

### #2531 FALLING FOR THE REBOUND BRIDE
*Wed in the West* • by Karen Templeton
When Emily Weber flees a broken engagement, she never expected to meet
her preteen crush in a New Mexico airport. But Colin Talbot is back and their
attraction is undeniable, despite the trauma he experienced while traveling as a
photographer. The timing couldn't be worse for a new relationship, but when fate
goes to that much trouble, maybe they should listen...

### #2532 HOW TO STEAL THE LAWMAN'S HEART
*Sweet Briar Sweethearts* • by Kathy Douglass
Widowed chief of police Trent Knight never expected Carmen Shields, the
woman he blames for his wife's death, to be the one to make him love again. Yet
Carmen is not only finding her way into his daughters' affections, she seems to
be stealing his heart, too.

---

**YOU CAN FIND MORE INFORMATION ON UPCOMING HARLEQUIN® TITLES,**
**FREE EXCERPTS AND MORE AT WWW.HARLEQUIN.COM.**

HSECNM0117

SPECIAL EXCERPT FROM

**H** HARLEQUIN®

## SPECIAL EDITION

*After a broken engagement, Emily Weber flees to her
cousin's peaceful New Mexico ranch and unexpectedly
finds herself drawn toward prodigal son Colin Talbot,
who can't wait to leave the first place Emily has ever
felt at home.*

Read on for a sneak preview of
**FALLING FOR THE REBOUND BRIDE,**
*the next book in Karen Templeton's*
**WED IN THE WEST** *miniseries.*

Wrapped more tightly in the shawl, she clomped across
the wooden porch, the sound then muffled in the dirt
as she made her way past the paddock to the foreman's
cabin. The clear, starry night was silent and still, save
for the thrum of crickets' chirping, the distant howl of
a coyote. The cabin's front door swung open before she
reached Colin's porch, a spear of light guiding her way.
And with that, the full ramifications of what she was
doing—or about to do, anyway—slammed into her.

But she had no idea what it might mean to Colin,
she thought as his broad-shouldered silhouette filled the
doorway, fragmenting the light. Maybe nothing, really—
oh, hell, her heart was about to pound right out of her
chest—since men were much more adept at these things
than women. Weren't they?

Spudsy scampered out onto the porch from behind
Colin's feet, wriggling up a storm when he saw her,
and Emily's heart stopped its whomping long enough to

squeeze at the sight of the bundle of furry joy she'd come to love.

At least she'd be able to keep the dog, she thought as she scooped up the little puppy to bury her face in his ruff, trying to ignore Colin's piercing gaze.

Oh, hell. That whole "sex as fun" thing? Who was she kidding? That wasn't her. Never had been. What on earth had made her think a single event would change *her*?

Although this one just might.

"I made a fire," Colin said quietly. Carefully. As though afraid she might spook. Never mind this had been her idea.

"That's nice."

*Ergh.*

Something like a smile ghosted around his mouth. "We can always just talk. No expectations. Isn't that what you said?" He shoved his hands into his pockets. "You're safe, honey. With me." His lips curved. "*From* me."

Still cuddling the puppy, she came up onto the porch. Closer. Too close. But not so close that she couldn't, if she were so inclined, still grab common sense by the hand and run like hell.

"And from myself?"

"That, I can't help you with."

Another step closer. Then another, each one a little farther away from common sense, whimpering in the dust behind her. "Kiss me," she whispered.

*Don't miss*
**FALLING FOR THE REBOUND BRIDE**
*by Karen Templeton,*
*available February 2017 wherever*
*Harlequin® Special Edition books and ebooks are sold.*

www.Harlequin.com

Copyright © 2017 by Karen Templeton-Berger

HSEEXP0117

**EXCLUSIVE LIMITED TIME OFFER AT**
# www.HARLEQUIN.com

$7.99 U.S./$9.99 CAN.

# $1.⁰⁰ OFF

*New York Times* Bestselling Author
## JODI THOMAS

In the heart of Ransom Canyon, sometimes the right match for a lonely soul is the one you least expect.

## WILD HORSE SPRINGS

*Available January 24, 2017!*
*Get your copy today!*

Receive **$1.00 OFF** the purchase price of
**WILD HORSE SPRINGS by Jodi Thomas**
**when you use the coupon code below on Harlequin.com**

## 1WILDHORSE

Offer valid from January 24, 2017 until February 28, 2017 on www.Harlequin.com. Valid in the U.S.A. and Canada only. To redeem this offer, please add the print or ebook version of WILD HORSE SPRINGS by Jodi Thomas to your shopping cart and then enter the coupon code at checkout.

**DISCLAIMER:** Offer valid on the print or ebook version of WILD HORSE SPRINGS by Jodi Thomas from January 24, 2017, at 12:01 a.m. ET until February 28, 2017, 11:59 p.m. ET at www.Harlequin.com only. The customer will receive $1.00 OFF the list price of WILD HORSE SPRINGS by Jodi Thomas in print or ebook on www.Harlequin.com with the **1WILDHORSE** coupon code. Sales tax applied where applicable. Quantities are limited. Valid in the U.S.A. and Canada only. All orders subject to approval.

® and ™ are trademarks owned and used by the trademark owner and/or its licensee.
© 2017 Harlequin Enterprises Limited

**HQN**™
**www.HQNBooks.com**

PHCOUPJT0217

**Join for FREE today at
www.HarlequinMyRewards.com**

Earn **FREE BOOKS** of your choice.

Experience **EXCLUSIVE OFFERS** and contests.

Enjoy **BOOK RECOMMENDATIONS**
selected just for you.

**PLUS!** Sign up now
and get **500** points
right away!

Earn
**FREE**
REWARDS
HarlequinMyRewards.com
Join
Today!

MYR16R

# THE WORLD IS BETTER WITH

## *Romance*

Harlequin has everything from contemporary, passionate and heartwarming to suspenseful and inspirational stories.

Whatever your mood, we have a romance just for you!

Connect with us to find your next great read, special offers and more.

**f** /HarlequinBooks

**🐦** @HarlequinBooks

www.HarlequinBlog.com

www.Harlequin.com/Newsletters

**◆ HARLEQUIN®**

A *Romance* FOR EVERY MOOD™

www.Harlequin.com

SERIESHALOAD2015